HELL ISLAND

STEVE METCALF

SEVERED PRESS
HOBART TASMANIA

HELL ISLAND

CHAPTER ONE

A COMMUNICATIONS MISHAP

THE SOUND WAS otherworldly. It was a mesh of teeth-rattling lows and blood-curdling highs. A deep roar resting atop a piercing screech. It came from a single beast. And the beast was right behind them. They all froze as their faceplate HUDs searched through the trees – an infrared and night-vision signal – for what had made the sound. Soon, the initial call was answered by a second. A bleating, frightened cry that put the first roar in context.

Call, answer.

Predator, prey.

Hunter, hunted.

The three researchers were safe, for now, but they had to get out of the war zone.

"This way," Anna said, speaking quietly over her mic and nodding her head in a particular direction. "South, southwest. Point-oh-three."

The other two men, along with the fourth member of the team still back at the facility, heard her quiet voice loud and clear over the faceplate speakers.

"Copy that," the two men in the field said almost simultaneously.

"It's almost dinner time," Anna said, before creeping off in the direction she had indicated. "And I don't want to be here when all hell breaks loose."

* *

In the control room, Davis Brighton was watching the action unfold. He was an older man by industry standards – well into his 50s – with graying hair around his temples and a shock of gray hair in his beard all across his chin. The rest of his hair was jet black and close cropped. As close cropped as his equipment would allow him to keep it.

One of the men, Nick Jennings, had simply let his beard grow for the last four months. It was starting to interfere with the negative pressure seal of his personal protective equipment, PPE, which included a hyper-technological faceplate that provided both fresh oxygen and a detailed heads-up display, HUD, across the visual field.

Davis stood in the control room of Facility Four – why it wasn't given a more creative name, he never understood. Facility Four was built by Allied Genetics on a peninsula with a wide expanse of earth removed to create a man-made island. Peninsula plus giant moat. The facility stood in a body of water that they believed would become the Black Sea. Eventually. It was a circular structure full of reinforced concrete and foot-thick acrylic windows. Collectively, it was miles ahead of any facility anywhere on Earth. That wasn't the most impressive part, though.

The facility existed 100 million years in the past.

In present day, Allied Genetics researchers had found a strange rift in time and space. By using a series of complex technical procedures, they were able to exploit this rift and send numerous teams of researchers, scientists and soldiers to explore the Cretaceous. In ancient Crimea they observed never-before-excavated dinosaurs and evidence of a super-ancient civilization.

Through a communications mishap, four researchers were left behind during a mission failure. The team had been sent to examine and, if possible, retrieve a mysterious energy signature tied to the ancient civilization – a group of buildings referred to as "The Ruins". The mission went south and the survivors made their way to the island. They must have been assumed dead, though, because no dedicated response team had ever come back for them. Now, four months later, they still hadn't given up hope of returning to modern civilization.

The four scientists had maintained a brain-storm list of ways to get back. Right now, they were looking for a rumored field supply storage box that might contain an emergency transponder.

Davis was providing as much overwatch as he could from Facility Four – referred to by the survivors and unofficial company documents as Hell Island.

* *

"South, southwest is confirmed," Davis said over the communication system. "You should be in the clear all the way to the target."

"Copy that," Anna said.

She had been elected the leader of this expedition. The team learned long ago that they would vote a field commander for each expedition so if decisions needed to be made, there would be one voice. Typically, the team acted democratically, but with one person in charge, it lessened the chance of dissent.

Anna was in her mid-thirties, tall and slim. Her heritage was Hispanic and she was a Tobin by marriage. She had been with Allied Genetics for three years and had made three trips back to Ancient Crimea through the rift. Her specialty was cryptozoology and reptilian reproduction. She wore what was left of her dark hair in a ponytail, and had only recently trimmed about six inches off the length.

She looked at the PDA-style computer screen that was mounted on her left wrist and started tapping in some instructions. It was a map showing their immediate area. She zoomed out to show their relation to the entrance to Hell Island – they were about a mile away.

Anna touched the screen at the moat and a green waypoint showed up. She scrolled a little further southwest on the map and there was a blinking red dot. This was the emergency supply depot they were after. The presumed location. A location that was planned, but they could find no proof at Facility Four that the depot was ever actually completed. They were after what could turn out to be a ghost.

But they had to try.

Anna pressed this location and a similar waypoint to the dock popped up on the screen. She linked her faceplate HUD to the wrist-mounted map. Her team was almost dead-center between the two points. One mile behind them was the bridge moat and one mile in front of them was the field supply storage box. She sent the updated map to her team via the local area network and looked back up into the dense jungle foliage.

"Let's boogie," she said, and they started off toward their goal.

* *

The Allied Genetics field-protective faceplate was a genius design using space-age materials and next-generation tech. It was a billion-dollar idea that was strictly kept in house for missions that required not only a protected oxygen supply but wireless connectivity to each node and multiple command servers.

Unfortunately, the billion-dollar idea belonged to TAKL Logistics. A company that now only exists via their Wikipedia page and has been called a myth by tech professionals and novices alike.

While Allied Genetics was built on the backbone of genius engineers, programmers and visionaries, it was equal parts a ruthless organization. Through their long history of success, they have left numerous crumpled companies in their wake. Some would say the assault on Objekt 221 was karma, but, truly, Allied was no different than any other business.

Now, Davis Brighton stood in one of the last remaining command centers of the company even though he didn't know about Allied's partial demise.

* *

In the field, Nick Jennings tapped the side of his faceplate. The seal around his face was fine although he had to ratchet up the negative pressure a little higher than normal to get a good connection. He had wanted to let his beard grow as some sort of good luck mojo. He had seen some professional football players do this over the course of a successful season ... for *some* reason.

Those athletes, unfortunately, didn't have to breathe oxygen out of a canister strapped to their chest. Nor did they have to maintain a perfect seal around a shield-shaped piece of personal protective gear or risk having their eyes bug out like the end of the movie, Total Recall.

The original.

In fact, TAKL Logistics had been developing the faceplate for use in both first responder and military applications. In both situations, the mocked-up instruction manual clearly stipulated the wearer had to maintain a close shave to ensure the proper connection.

"Damn," Jennings said to himself, although it was picked up by the faceplate's mic.

"What's that?" Arlington Beech said.

They were all three making a beeline toward the glowing red icon Anna had put on their maps. Arlington walked directly behind Jennings and saw the man reach up and rub the side of his faceplate. He knew the beard would be going away if they made it back to Hell Island.

Jennings, a 42-year old man with dual advanced degrees from UCLA in computer sciences, was having the exact same thought.

There was a blip on the HUD of his faceplate indicating they had arrived at their destination.

"We're here, Davis," Anna said.

The three researchers lined up directly in front of the steel box. It was the size of a large closet measuring a six-foot square but was only three feet high. There was a small access door in the center of the unit. Anna, Nick and Art all stood facing the small door. There had been a lock securing the door, but it had long since disappeared. There were deep, menacing scrapes running diagonally across where the lock would have been.

Three of them.

They were claw marks made by something strong enough to destroy the surface of a stainless-steel box and shred the padlock that held it closed.

"Oh boy," Anna said.

* *

Arlington Beech's breath deflector malfunctioned. It was a strangely regular occurrence and no amount of minor surgery to the faceplate seemed to clear the glitch. Anna had some medical training and did a cursory examination of his face with the entire team looking on. She had shrugged – he remembered this clearly – and pulled off her latex gloves with a snap.

"Something about his lips," she had said, sitting up straight in her chair with Art reclined in a desk chair. Both Davis and Nick nodded.

"Yeah," Nick said. "He's got weird lips."

"Okay, that's enough," Art said as he pulled his chair up to the seated position. "I'm not sure how much help I was expecting to get from you three. But, you can all kiss my acreage."

The memory evaporated as quickly as it had started. Absently, Beech rubbed his outer faceplate to clear the fogged portion of the acrylic screen. Of course, with the fog on the inside, his gloved fingers did nothing.

Anna had bent to examine the claw marks against the door.

"Are you getting this, Davis?"

Over the faceplate comms, Davis answered in the affirmative. Back at Facility Four, he was leaning in closer to the monitor that displayed Anna's camera.

"They don't look uniform, though," he continued into the microphone. "Maybe an axe or a claw-hammer."

"But that would mean ..." Nick said and then a warning popped up on his HUD. The other two researchers looked at him. He looked around frantically. It wasn't a proximity alarm; it was a pressure alarm from his faceplate and breathing apparatus. "Damn," he said, quickly reaching up his hands and pressing them against the faceplate, physically forcing it against his skin.

"You idiot," Arlington said.

"You shave when you get back," Anna said. "No buts."

"Yes, ma'am," Nick said.

With a final disapproving tsk, Anna turned back to the small, unlocked, door. She knelt and pushed it open.

* *

Empty.

"Seriously?" Anna said into her faceplate. According to the standard manifest, the documentation called this an *emergency field re-supply station*. There should be six sets each of weapons, replacement faceplates, oxygen canisters, provisions and an extra flare gun. There should also be a ...

"Wait," Davis said from the control room. "Anna, to your left. Turn to the left."

She did as was suggested and looked to the left of the open door. Mounted on the wall was a large, complex handheld computer. It looked like an abnormally thick computer tablet but with a bunch of extra face knobs and dials.

"Gotcha," Anna said, pulling it off the hook on the wall. She stood back up and the door swung shut under its own weight. "Are you sure this is going to work?"

Art nodded.

"It's an ion-dormant battery charge," he said. "It's designed to sit like this without being charged for about three years. You'll need to prime it. Like an emergency weather radio." He paused for a beat and then pointed. "There's a little crank on the right side. Give it a few spins and it should turn on."

At the Hell Island facility, Davis Brighton was flipping through a procedure manual.

"He's right," he said into the microphone that broadcast to the team comm channel. "Spin the crank eight or ten times and then power the unit on. When it lights up, you'll hit the button on the face that says BROADCAST. It's a blue button. It'll send a signal to whoever's listening on the emergency channel."

"Alright," Anna said, leaning back against the squat building with a watchful eye into the forest all around her. They were losing sunlight and she wanted to end this mission as quickly as she could. Nick, she figured, would soon get tired of holding his own face to prevent choking to death in the poisonous air. With a final look around the forest floor and up to the canopy, she turned around and the two researchers crowded in behind her. "Here we go."

Anna cranked the lever on the side of the heavily-built machine. She knew it was essentially a computer but that it had been over-engineered so that it more resembled a sturdy construction or military-grade piece of electronics. When she finished creating a charge for the dormant battery, the machine beeped and powered itself on. She was startled, but turned the crank twice more.

"Okay," Art said. "It's on."

"Right," Anna said and stopped the repetitive motion.

There was a four-inch screen at the top half of the unit and several rows of buttons and knobs that filled in the rest of the machine. Centered, right beneath the small LCD screen, was a blue button. It was highlighted. BROADCAST.

"The *broadcast* button is the emergency signal, right?" she asked the team in general.

Art was nodding his head over her left shoulder. Davis, however, answered vocally from Facility Four.

"Yes," he said over the faceplate comms. "Hit it and get out of there. I see a couple of signals heading your way. They're not on the path, but they might accidentally find you."

"Copy that," Anna said.

She braced the machine against her hip with her left hand at the top of it. She reached down with her right hand and pressed the button with her index finger. The machine emitted a flash and a small *crack* sound and the screen lit up with a dull glow. It spelled out the word and cycled back to the beginning.

B ... R ... O ... A ... D ... C ... A ... S ... T ... I ... N ... G ...
B ... R ... O ...

"Alright," Nick said, shockingly unmuffled even though he was physically crushing his faceplate to his face. "Let's get the hell outta here."

* *

Arlington "Art" Beech was the youngest of the researchers who had been trapped at Hell Island. The Other. Ancient Crimea. Earth minus 100 million years. He was 29 years old and recently had been working as a paleontologist. He was an apprentice of Dr. Taylor "Tate" McKenna out of San Diego and had been rising up the ranks. Art had received a glowing review from Ms. McKenna after which Allied Genetics snapped him up. He was a brilliant researcher with a knowledge of this subject matter. He had also proved himself somewhat of a computer whiz as he helped their systems maintain some reliability even in the face of four months with no regular updates from the mothership computers.

Most of the missions he went on, he brought something of a forced bravado to the group. A young energy that was a valuable blend of caution and optimism. Right now, though, he was worried about Nick.

The two had grown close. A psychological effect of their situation. Forced brotherhood. Generally, something like that could flip either way. It could force people together or it could force them apart. In this scenario, the two had become close friends.

Nick would have to shave that ridiculous beard. Possibly shave his head for good measure. And pull a new faceplate out of their reserve stock.

First, however, they would have to get out of the jungle and back to their island fortress. As if on cue, Art's faceplate proximity alarm went off. In unison, all three researchers looked around to help their system identify the dinosaurs.

"I don't have a clear picture over here," Davis said. "And I really don't want to know. Long-range telemetry puts them at Gamma-Class Predators. Unclassified. Gives them a designation of UC-223X. The X because we haven't had a master update. Three of them."

"I got them," Anna said. The other two men turned to look in the direction she had turned. All three faceplates lit up at the same time with highlights of the three predators. They were designated by the main computer as A, B, C after the main categorization. A forward-thinking program. That way, when one member of the team said something about predator A, everyone knew which one he or she was referring to.

Nick looked at the small concrete building.

"Run or hide?" he asked.

* *

Since day one at Facility Four, the team had committed to a physical fitness regimen. There was no shortage of food ... both healthy and processed ... but they wanted to push each other to exercise. It was some sort of latent predator-prey response. Something akin to "I need to be stronger than the thing attacking me."

They used the United States Army's Basic Combat Training regimen metrics as a benchmark for all things fitness related. The number of push-ups, sit-ups, pull-ups, etc. they could do in a minute. The team had found three treadmills and worked out daily to ensure they had endurance.

Right now, they would test it.

They should be able to easily jog two miles in 20 minutes, maintaining a speed close to four miles per hour over relatively smooth terrain. They could run the same distance in about half the time – 12 minutes – at a speed of about nine miles per hour.

It was an unclassified predator so they didn't have a clear indication of its land-speed. The goal wasn't to outrun it, but to get away before it knew they were there.

Their uniforms were a dark green, designed to blend into the environment, and carried a neutral chemical smell. Similar to a common flower that grew in that region. To most animals, they were invisible. Possibly, they looked like a moving plant.

They had made it the first mile in a little more than five minutes and then disaster struck.

Nick had been running with one hand on his face attempting to correct the negative-pressure disagree while pumping the other arm in time with the corresponding leg. It had thrown his balance off a bit, but he was doing okay with Anna in front and Art in back.

For their part, the three UC predators had remained cautiously engaged with the three fleeing researchers. More than anything, they were simply curious where the three flowers were heading. Predation, generally, required the conservation of energy, so they were slowly loping along at a safe distance. That is, until one of the flowers fell as an animal would.

Nick tripped.

He tripped on a thick root that was partially hidden in fallen leaves and other detritus. He stumbled, tripped against Anna's feet and fell against a large tree to his left. Even in his panic, he didn't remove his left hand from his faceplate – which probably didn't help his balance in going to the ground. Art Beech stopped to help his friend up. Anna regained her balance and paused to assess the situation. She didn't need to say anything as Davis came over their comms.

"Team," he said. "Let's go. Swarming behavior. You're about to get flanked. Thirty seconds."

Everyone's proximity alarms were screaming a warning. Anna could see the three UC predators as highlighted images on her HUD. She could see B split apart from A and C. All three researchers pulled their submachine guns, SMGs, from modified hip holsters. They had enlarged trigger guards to account for their enviro-suit gloves and a light blue laser sight designed to show up against the green foliage. Two of the UCs bounded up behind them and stopped, assessing the situation. The final UC, UC-B, was still flanking them from the trees.

The faceplate computer was quickly making calculations and displaying a readout. The two unclassified predators were around 40 inches in height and weighed in at an estimated 120 pounds. They looked lithe and quick. Sort of a cross between a Compsognathus and a Velociraptor popularized in movies and as a mascot for a professional sports team. They were both standing on their hind legs and swaying gently from side to side, balanced by a long, thick tail. In the fading light, the researchers could see the reptiles were a dark green color with a blast of bristles along the top of their heads. It was something approximating hair and stood nearly half a foot high. The two UCs had colorful diamond patterns that ran down the length of their spines. The patterns were similar, but the coloring was different. It could have been akin to fingerprints or eye color. A unique personal identifier. The reptile on the right had a predominantly brown and yellow pattern while the reptile on the left had mostly shades of blue running down the length of his back.

Anna, like she had been in the past, was struck by the vibrant colors this ancient world had to offer.

Art held his weapon in his left hand with an outstretched arm. He offered his right hand to help Nick regain his footing. His heavy, panicked breathing was causing a layer of foggy moisture along the bottom third of his faceplate. The two UCs stood in the path the three researchers had just run along. This standoff was taking place just under a mile away from the moat and entrance to Facility Four.

A voice, quiet and calm, came over the faceplate speakers.

"Art," Davis said. "You have the third UC approaching three o'clock."

Four things happened, then, in rapid succession.

One, Arlington Beech snapped his head to the right to get a clear reading of the third UC's position.

Two, the UC with the brown and yellow coloring saw this as a moment of opportunity and bounded forward to attack the distracted prey.

Three, Art saw this action in his peripheral vision even as the faceplate identified the third dinosaur out in the trees. He fired his weapon at the approaching reptile.

Four, he hit the approaching beast with a three-round burst of fire – all three shots hitting center mass. The small dino went down in a heap.

After those, a fifth event occurred – and it was bad for all involved. The third UC came bounding out of the jungle to the team's right and flashed across the small path into the jungle to the team's left. This all happened as the yellow-striped reptile was falling to the ground in a bleeding heap. The team of researchers had a flash of purple coloring, an open mouth full of razor-sharp teeth, and then screams.

The creature had departed as quickly as he had appeared. Unfortunately, he took Art's left arm into the jungle with him.

* *

Warning klaxons were going off in all three field researchers' masks as well as the main control room of Facility Four.

Davis, removed from the battle, could remain somewhat clear-headed.

"Protective foam," he shouted into the microphone which was amplified in his team's faceplate speakers. "Anna, protective foam in the wound."

Nick was firing back and forth from the dying UC to the one who disappeared behind the tree line at 9 o'clock. The other UC had backed off and to the side, away from the three researchers. The odds were now against him, even if his mate came back from the jungle, they were – at this point – outnumbered. Nick had now totally risen to his feet and was firing with his right hand, and his left was holding his faceplate flush to his head. His SMG gave a warning click click click sound and he knew his magazine was about to run dry.

Anna had pulled a canister out of a small Velcro pocket on the left thigh of her eco suit. She ran to Art and popped the top of the metal tube. He was silent, in shock, lying prone on the jungle floor. His eco suit had sealed internally at the shoulder joint. He was breathing shallowly.

"It's okay, man," Anna said. "It's okay, Art. You're going to be fine."

She pressed the over-sized nozzle of the metal tube and a sticky, medicated foam came out. It was a disinfecting and cauterizing agent all in one and was used to protect anything from a laceration to a gunshot wound. She wasn't sure if it had ever been used to seal an amputation, but they were going to try.

"Get him to his feet," Davis said over the comms.

"He's gone into shock," Anna said, hearing the click-clack of Nick changing the clip of his weapon. She could hear Art wheezing into the comms, as the red warning lights of his HUD illuminated his face. "Oh, God. I think he's passed out."

"Probably from blood loss," Brighton said from the relative comfort of Facility Four. "I'm coming out there."

"You stay where you are," Anna said. She crouched over Art in a protective stance and raised her gun. The second UC had joined the first and stood a ways away from them, facing the researchers. Two against two.

"I'm sorry," Davis said. "You've got three more incoming. Same signal. Same UC. Designated D, E, F."

The bleeding UC finally died with a death rattle – a violent shiver ran down his back and then he lay still. The two remaining reptiles of his pack looked to him, each other, and then off to the jungle. In the direction of D, E and F, who at that moment, burst from the relative protection of the jungle overgrowth. The three new beasts erupted from the tree line between the fallen UC and the three researchers. The new three pounced on the fallen Art and one ripped his faceplate off. Immediately, Beech began convulsing. Both Anna and Nick were thrown back in shock as D's tail was whipping back and forth in a defensive maneuver.

"Get out of there," Davis said over the comm system. "Even if you beat them, more will come."

"We can't leave him here," Anna said, scrambling backward and getting to her feet – SMG at the ready.

"I'm tracking something big," Davis said. "It might be coming to check out the commotion. The long range says it might be a T-rex."

Suddenly, they had an opening. The two remaining UCs from the original pack advanced on the three new dinos. The three designated as D, E, and F turned away from the two researchers and stood in defensive positions against both the fallen scientist and the fallen UC.

The five predators were going to fight over the spoils of war.

"Let's go," Anna said, grabbing Nick under the right arm.

He adjusted the grip of his hand against his faceplate and ran off after her.

CHAPTER TWO

MURKY

ANGUS POPE WAS an explosion of a man. He stood well north of six feet tall and weighed in just one big lunch shy of three hundred pounds. He was the AI department head of tech company Precision Robotics – but managed to keep aware of every project going on throughout the organization. Based on his position within the company and the fact that it was his turn in the rotation, he was shouldering the management responsibilities of the company's Anvil Canyon facility – Objekt 221.

Precision Robotics had been taking advantage of the legal murkiness and the general corporate disruption of their main global competitor – Allied Genetics.

Four months ago, Precision had embarked on a form of corporate espionage that ultimately uncovered decades of data showing that Allied had run dozens of immoral and illegal experiments. They were ready to go public and shut the organization down when they also found that Allied was holding hostage a group of scientists who had uncovered evidence of an ancient civilization by going through a time rift into Ancient Crimea – 100 million years into Earth's past.

One of the scientists being held against their will was a former Precision employee named Damon Butcher. The corporate espionage had turned personal.

Using a hired paramilitary force known only as the Wraiths, Precision Robotics rescued the scientists and executed a hostile takeover of the Objekt 221 facility – and with it, the time portal into the Cretaceous.

Murky.

Since then, Precision had been rotating department heads to oversee a data mining operation at Allied's former facility while they took the time to figure out what they were going to do about the dinosaur data.

* *

Angus was eating lunch and trying to work at the same time. He had heated up a bowl of canned pasta and was spooning large mouthfuls while reading through printed documents and comparing data to the computer screen. He was in a sub-control room labeled "COMM4" and his team was trying to put together a log of movements in the months prior to the assault on Anvil Canyon.

Something in the personnel files wasn't adding up.

Suddenly, there was a trill from a computer across the room. It was a polite sound that actually made Angus pick up his phone and activate the screen. The alert was so unassuming that it might have been a notification regarding an online purchase. There was nothing on his screen and the AI-head looked around the room.

He was alone in COMM4. The room was a 12x12-foot square with three long desks of computers. All told, there were seven computer workstations in the room. The six on the long tables and the one in the back of the room that Angus had been working at. The front of the room was a whiteboard covered in numbers and notes.

After 30 seconds, the sound chimed again.

Angus stood up and looked around the room. Save for the one he had been working on, all of the computers were in sleep mode, but they were all on. The ambient noise of the room was basically half a dozen computer fans pulsing in tandem. He took four steps which brought his bulk into the center of the room. Angus stood silently, waiting for the trill.

Beep-a-beep-ehmm-beep.

"There," he said to himself, cocking his head to the side.

The sound seemed to come from the front-most row of computers – the workstation on the far right.

He walked over and sat down at that specific unit and nudged the wireless mouse to the right of the keyboard. The screen came to life. Angus looked around the now-active desktop to see if there was a visual alert that accompanied the sound. There was.

"What the …?" he said to himself as he pushed the onscreen cursor to a small blue bubble in the lower-right corner. The white text on the bubble said **BEACON ACTIVE**.

* *

They were close in age and IQ, but generally, that's where the similarities ended. Damon Butcher and Cadey Park enjoyed each other's company, but they didn't share much in the way of similar backgrounds, educational interests, entertainment interests or professional accreditation. Having said that, they got along well and together formed the backbone of one of Precision Robotics' newest advanced work groups. So new, in fact, that it didn't really even have a name yet. There was some bizarre number/letter combination in the HR computer so that everyone kept getting paid … but their boss, Angus Pope, hadn't even named the group. Anything more concrete than Shared AI, at least.

"I thought the idea was that the moon had cracked off the surface of the Earth and formed into a sphere while in orbit." Damon was working through a thick stack of binders in the first quadrant of the document lab. This was their assignment on this rotation. They were given a room full of information and told to summarize, collate and synthesize it. Basically, to look for anything interesting that Allied had been working on up until their catastrophic failure at the hands of the Wraith paramilitary group.

Murky.

"That, the dent in the Earth where the Pacific Ocean is now – that's where the moon used to be."

Cadey didn't even bother looking up from her own binder. She flipped another page while shaking her head disapprovingly.

"That's the *fission theory* and it's more than a century old. Was disproved a couple of generations ago. When we could accurately measure the age of the moon versus the oceanic crust." She flipped another page and then looked up. "Man, you really don't follow this kind of stuff, do you?"

Damon shook his head.

"Talk to me about movies, video games or muscle cars," he said. "I told you I didn't really have any lunar discussion points. It's not like I was intentionally misleading you."

Damon, in his mid-thirties, had been tapped to run the Theoretical Biometrics division at Precision Robotics before being recruited over to Allied Genetics. They were after not only his brain, but his military training – Army Force Recon. He was sent back on two missions to Ancient Crimea through O221's time rift. From the second excursion team, only he and Cadey survived the final mission – a combination of dinosaurs and the murderous Jason Beale who was out to protect company secrets. Now, back at PR, Damon was happy to be working with Cadey in a new team under his old mentor, Angus Pope.

"No, no and no," Cadey said. "I mean, my personal favorite theory is Theia."

She waited for Damon to respond, but he simply shrugged at her in a *go on if you want to* gesture.

Which she did.

"You know," she continued. "A planet about the size of Mars comes rampaging through the Milky Way, blasts right into a young Earth and shears off a ton of material. This material continues in orbit around her mom and eventually combines to form the moon as we know it. The collision also caused the weird tilted axis which gives us our seasons. Could even be the reason for the Chandler Wobble."

"You know, there's actually a guy *inside* that suit of armor called Iron Man," Damon offered. "It's not a robot."

Cadey sighed and went back to her binder.

Cadey Park, likewise, was in her mid-thirties but had defected from North Korea in her teens. As a National Math Champion, she was afforded a certain amount of uncharacteristic autonomy and used it to escape the regime. She took up cryptozoology – Damon's primary degree – as a hobby just to mess with him.

"Be that as it may," Damon finally said. "There's something cool about the idea that the moon was once a part of the Earth – not just some separate body."

Cadey smiled.

"I agree," she said.

* *

Beacon Active.

"What beacon?" Angus asked himself. The computer monitor in front of him was active and he had rested his hands in the HOME position on the small, silver keyboard. He didn't even remember doing it – it was just a habit that someone who worked with computers naturally picked up. You see a keyboard and you automatically rest your fingers in the starting position. Bump the mouse to wake up the screen and get ready to type. Angus sat for a moment, squinting at the computer screen.

The small visual indicator was in the lower right portion of the screen and the rest of the screen was blank of activity. The wallpaper was an HD image of a lush, green forest with the highly stylized lettering and logo of Allied Genetics stretched across the top. There were a few shortcuts and a few pinned tasks. Nothing that jumped out at him.

In his rotations through O221, Angus had explored most of the common systems fairly extensively. Out of curiosity, he leaned to his left, to the next computer workstation and bumped the mouse. He looked at the newly-activated screen to see if the same "Beacon Active" notification appeared there.

"Huh," he said to the empty room. "Not there."

He came back to his own monitor and shrugged. Angus grabbed the mouse and brought the cursor to the small blue icon. There was no rollover state and nothing happened when he right-clicked to examine any options.

"Well, let's see."

* *

The small blue bubble expanded into its own application window. It was a white border with a black interior and yellow text. Lines and lines of text filled the entire application window like some sort of command-prompt readout. There were three blank spaces and then a long line of numbers along the bottom. The last bit of text was 18:10:00.

"Okay," Angus said. He leaned in toward the monitor and scanned through each line of text three times, looking for patterns. Nothing was immediately discernable.

18:15:00

"Interesting," he said.

None of the rest of the text on the page had changed except the last bit. That string of numbers had increased by 5. Also, the long line of numbers and letters immediately preceding it had changed.

"Time," Angus muttered.

He kept reading through the dense page of text to see if anything else had changed. He couldn't see any new or altered strings until he got to the very end. Again, the last three lines changed.

18:20:00

"And a beacon," he said, leaning back in his chair. The small desk chair groaned under the AI head's bulk. "Beacon active," he said, recalling the original notification on the computer monitor. "Now, there's a string of text changing, presumably, every five minutes. Time and," he trailed off. "Location. It's giving me coordinates. Refreshed every five minutes."

Angus crossed his arms against his chest and furrowed his brow.

"That makes sense. But what are you trying to tell me?"

His eyes ran up and down the huge block of text that made up 90 percent of the application window. Squinted. Exhaled. Leaned back in closer to the monitor. He started searching around the computer programs for what he was looking for and opened up a new application next to the yellow text of the beacon.

It was similar to a search algorithm, but designed mostly to identify mystery documents. It was included in most operating systems as an auto-feature, but could be opened to find even more functions. There was no name on the authorship, just a company that no longer existed – a company that had been swallowed up by a larger Silicon Valley company and then a larger one and then a larger one more than a decade ago. Angus was happy to find the little program because he had written the original code and knew all of the extra fun stuff he could do with it.

With a series of keystrokes, he pulled the beacon information into the little program called Mag-Nit.

"Ah," Angus said. "It's an image file. What, though? A map to trace the beacon coordinates?"

The program ran, a small, spinning wheel showing its progress. When the readout completed, there was a small button with the text MORE INFO at the bottom of the screen. Angus moved the cursor over to the button and clicked it. The screen immediately changed.

"Oh boy," he said.

* *

Damon and Cadey were still in the document lab. They had finished the first quadrant over the course of the week and had, now, moved to the second. Their whiteboard was covered in notes and they had started working on the second one – on the west wall. They had just settled into the first binder of documentation when Angus came in.

He was holding two sheets of printed paper and had a wry smile on his face. In his other hand, he held a small computer tablet – the likes of which were all over this facility, as well as other Precision Robotics labs world-wide. PR tended to use them for locked functions, but Allied seemed to have kept most of theirs in full-computer mode.

Angus took a few steps into the room and stood next to the small café table Damon had brought into the room to work at.

"Something interesting," Angus said. He had folded the two sheets of paper and clipped them to the back of the computer tablet with his left hand. With his right, he started typing on the tablet screen while leaning in toward the table. Cadey and Damon crowded around him.

"The ED-C10," Angus said, reading the information off his hand-held tablet. "An ion-dormant, field-enabled beacon. Static or mobile. Designed for material or personnel extraction. Used experimentally at Tech Overlook before the patent was acquired by Allied Genetics five years ago. They were used sparingly and recently discontinued for unknown reasons. I assume they were going to integrate the tech into the next hardware release of the field-protective faceplate. They were pulled out of the field and placed in storage."

"Okay," Damon said in the silent moment.

"I checked and there are five unaccounted for," Angus continued. "One of them went active about 30 minutes ago."

"Okay?" Cadey continued Damon's thought.

"In dino-land."

* *

They were all three silent for a moment. It was clear that Angus had already reached his conclusion. He was letting Damon and the new girl, Cadey Park, catch up to him. They were both geniuses in their fields and a little mental exercise – a lateral thinking puzzle – wasn't a waste of time in the least.

"One of the missing units malfunctioned?" Damon asked. "Software glitch or hardware, perhaps? Maybe some moisture got inside and shorted the unit out?"

"Good call," Angus said. "That was my first thought, too. I pulled up the design specs and the instruction manual." He set the computer tablet down on the table in front of the two other PR employees. They both glanced at it as Angus continued to talk. "The battery is dormant and needs a charge to fire up. Like a piece of emergency gear. You have to crank a handle or something."

"Oh, yeah, I see," Cadey said, pointing to a portion of the diagram on the screen.

"Reading those documents," Angus continued as he spun the little computer around to switch digital pages, "I came across an interesting nugget." He turned the tablet around to face Cadey and Damon once again. Now, he unfolded the two sheets of printer paper. He placed the first on the table flanking one side of the tablet. "Here is the start-up signal for the beacon. Whole bunch of text with the time and coordinates at the very bottom."

Angus paused as he tapped the bottom three lines of text with his right index finger.

"On screen," he continued, "the coordinates update every five minutes so you can track the beacon. This up here, though," he said, tapping the blob of text that made up the greater portion of the print-out.

"Oh my God," Damon said, looking up in shock from the computer tablet to Angus. "What was it?"

Angus smiled. Cadey kept reading for a moment and then looked up as well.

"It's a strange feature, right?" Angus said, smiling. "There's a little camera on the front of the ED-C10. I'm not sure what its actual function is, but it's designed to take a picture of whoever activates the unit. Possibly, it's a security measure."

He unfolded the second sheet of paper and put it on the table, on the other side of the computer tablet. It was on the opposite side from the printed sheet of numbers so he could reference both at the same time.

They could see three individuals – all wearing field-operative gear including the protective face plate. There was a woman in the center of the frame, flanked by two men – one seemed to be holding his mask in place. They were clearly Allied Genetics researchers.

"Apparently, there are three people trying to reach out to us from Ancient Crimea," Angus said, smiling again. "The Cretaceous. Right here at this very location. Only … 100 million years ago."

CHAPTER THREE

GEOGRAPHICAL FEATURES ARE A FORCE MULTIPLIER

IT DIDN'T BELONG there. Some sort of concrete and steel pyramid in the middle of a swath of North Dakota farmland. The pyramidal shape was blunted, however, with the top 15 percent missing and the four sides capping off with a wide, flat roof about 45 feet into the air. Spiked with antennas and other communications structures of various function, the shape seemed squat from a distance but continued to grow to mammoth proportions as individuals approached.

The Nekoma Pyramid.

And the Wraiths were coming.

**

It was retro to call them a mercenary force, but that was truly what they were. Sergott Solutions was a global conglomeration offering bodyguards and other private security forces for events, parties, political gatherings – whatever the client needed. Last month, they were called upon to provide security for a Sweet 16 birthday celebration in Des Moines, Iowa, for example. For the right price, there was always a solution.

When matters became more militaristic, Sergott employed a battalion of retired troops from all over the world. From U.S. Army Rangers to British SAS, this group of combatants were called the Wraiths and they were prepared to resolve any conflict in any locale.

Right now, they were descending upon North Dakota in the dead of night.

There were two advance teams of four men each, one overwatch on digital remote and one trail team – for support only – of four more men. The two advance teams had jokingly called the start of this mission *parachuting onto a pyramid in the middle of a corn field.* They weren't entirely wrong.

* *

Adjacent to Nekoma, North Dakota, the Stanley R. Mickelsen Safeguard Complex was truly a sight to behold. Acres of flat land dominated by a giant concrete pyramid – it was the epitome of Cold War spending and non-utilization. The facility, built as an advanced missile-detection radar array with a host of defensive firepower, was meant to detect a Russian attack coming toward the United States from the vast Canadian tundra. Unfortunately, almost as soon as the facility was completed, it was rendered obsolete by new treaties and new technology.

Abandoned since the 1970s, the facility had now been taken over by a small, rogue militia group. They were called the Defenders of the Pure and had broken off from a larger group, Clarke's Boys, a year prior. The Defenders of the Pure had stumbled upon the Nekoma Pyramid shortly after declaring their organizational independence and had made it their own. The area was largely a tourist attraction – people, in their astonishment, taking photos of the visual imbalance – but the DOTP had discovered something.

The facility was as deep as it was tall.

And there were hidden treasures.

* *

During a period of excess in the '80s, the Safeguard Complex had been used as a way-station. A storage facility for obsolete material. And then it was forgotten yet again. The DOTP had stumbled upon the off-the-books tourist attraction in 2014 and used it for a meeting area after they split from Clarke's Boys. In their exploration, they found pallets of material that had been on its way to a garment facility, reams of paper for dot-matrix printers and rooms full of similar supplies. Things that probably would have been useful further along whatever production process they were set upon – 30 years prior.

There was one wooden crate, though, that seemed to defy explanation. There was no documentation – only a part number stenciled in paint on the side of the crate. Every few months, someone in the group decided to find the part number on the Internet and finally learn what the machine was. It was associated with the date 1998, but that was as far as they could get.

It looked like a diesel generator with three computers bolted to it. No one could figure out what it was, what it did or even how to turn it on.

The Wraiths, however, had been hired to extract the unit. Personnel collateral damage to the Defenders of the Pure was acceptable. And encouraged.

* *

"So, we're being sent in blind with a 70-year old blueprint?" the field commander assigned to team Theta spoke softly against his throat mic.

The man he was speaking to, Jimmie Granville, had the callsign "Walnuts" and was the on-site support for the digital remote overwatch. It was his job to assess the situation and turn over control to the remote. In this situation, however, there seemed to be little he could do.

"Yes sir," Walnuts said, quietly. "They have a surveillance system in the facility, but it's fairly primitive. And totally closed-loop."

"Hmm," the commander, Alex Scott – callsign "Beef" – replied. He began scrolling through the digital blueprints on his wrist-mounted computer. Each of the Wraith soldiers wore a highly advanced piece of machinery on their left forearm. It was basically a digital gauntlet that had a computer monitor on it. It was a way the team could communicate with each other – redundant to the throat mics – as well as share more complex information. Right now, Beef had stopped on one of the more recent maps the team had access to. He had scrolled out to view the village of Nekoma and the Safeguard Complex. One line, highlighted in neon green, connected the two areas. He made a swiping motion and the image was shared to all of the Wraith team.

"Could you piggyback a utility line?" the commander asked. "Phone? Electrical monitoring? Weather survey?" As he said this, two additional neon lines appeared on the map – one blue and one green. There were three utility service lines highlighted on the blueprint.

"It might work, sir," Walnuts said, nodding. "Back in five."

Granville hustled off to splice a service line so they could get some sort of intel on the interior of the building before breeching.

"Blindness is a force multiplier," came a voice over the earpiece. It was the commander of the other field team. Rick "Ahab" Everson was in charge of team Ice – nearly a mile away on the diagonal portion of the facility map from Commander Scott.

The two men had worked together numerous times and their "brother soldier" relationship had extended very near the neighborhood of "friend." They had fun ribbing each other, to the point that when they were together in the field, they had to name their force teams from completely separate rubrics. While a normal op might have Team Fire and Team Ice, or Team Alpha and Team Beta, Ahab was just as likely to lobby for a car name and Beef would choose a color. They did this because similar mission team names could be construed as one above the other and they preferred to be seen as equals.

"Geographical features are a force multiplier," Scott said. "If we don't have any idea of the entrenched environment, it's the Hot Gates all over again."

"My fearsome reputation is a force multiplier," Ahab said and laughed. "Out."

"Yes, thank you. Over and out. Walnuts, status?"

"Found the communication line, sir," came the response over Scott's earpiece. "Splicing the remote in now."

"Copy that," Beef said and then went silent.

"Hot Gates?" came the voice of Theta's newest team member, Dustin Riggs, callsign "Mini." He was so-named partly because of his short stature and partly in reference to the Austin Powers movie franchise. Riggs was often referred to as the Mini Me of Rick "Ahab" Everson. Outside of height, they shared a general body type and facial structure. They could be brothers.

"You forget your ROTC already, rookie?" Beef said, smiling and checking his tech in the final minutes before their assault. "The Hot Gates? The Battle of Thermopylae? A small force of Greek soldiers holds off the advance of a vastly superior number of Persian aggressors?"

Mini nodded.

"Ah," he said. "The movie *300*."

Beef visibly shuddered.

"Sure. The Hollywood-action-movie version of the story," he said. "In reality about 1,000 troops – both Spartan and Thespian – formed a rear guard to thwart the Persian advance of more than 100,000 soldiers while the rest of the Greek army retreated to prepare a better defense. The rear guard was eventually annihilated but it took a week and the Persians suffered enormous losses."

There was a pause as a crackle of static enveloped their earpieces. It was a quarter-second burst of interference from the remote satellite link-up that Walnuts had initiated.

"Logged in and turning control over to Remote Overwatch," Walnuts said on the comm link.

"Control accepted, Theta. Downloading live feed," Overwatch said.

All the members of both Ice and Theta looked at their gauntlet computers at the same time. There was a slight blink and the blueprint that had previously taken up the monitor minimized and was replaced by a live video feed from one of the Safeguard Complex's solid-state surveillance cameras.

"Running resolution algorithms," Overwatch said. "I count six active cameras and two inactive. Building a map of the opposing force. Looks like we have a minimum of 30 troopers. Four in sentry position. I'm not seeing any signs of entrenchment. No active defense."

"Copy that, Overwatch," Ahab said. "We move in 30."

"Copy that," Beef said. "You see, Mini, a force multiplier is any element that acts to your advantage in battle. Gives you a larger presence than you would have standing in a wheat field shooting at each other like they would have in any battle earlier than, say, 1800. Eight versus 30. The element of surprise is *our* force multiplier. It makes us bigger and badder than we actually are."

* *

From above, the Nekoma Pyramid looked like a diamond situated with its points matching up perfectly with the points of a compass. There were two underground access tunnels – one extending from the eastern point and one extending from the southern. Team Theta would access the southern tunnel and Ice would advance through the eastern.

Based on the remote overwatch and the information Walnuts had given them from the utility line hack, the two teams would meet on the third sub-level, the ultimate control room of the Safeguard

Complex. From there, having eliminated all opposition, they would locate and remove the mission objective.

* *

Overwatch had piggy-backed the surveillance array signal but there was little else he could do. The team faced a technology gap akin to attempting to control a 1980s-era television with this year's most popular smartphone. Impossible to accomplish.

Armed with a live feed of 75 percent of the Nekoma Pyramid, both Wraith teams advanced along their prospective spines of the capital-Y-shaped tunnel system.

Alex "Beef" Scott took Theta along the southern-most expanse. There were two enemy combatants stationed midway down the tunnel. They had erected a loose blockade of boxes and storage crates from which to adopt a defensive position. Unfortunately for them, right now, one sentry was asleep and the other was staring at his phone screen with rapt attention.

"Silent," Beef said under his breath. "Blades."

His two advance men responded with "Copy" and pulled identical KA-BAR combat knives out of thigh scabbards. They traversed the final 20 yards in utter silence and near-complete darkness largely due to the spotty maintenance of the corridor lighting system.

The two men attacked in tandem but the cell phone soldier went down first simply due to positioning. The sleeping sentry uttered a GURKH sound as he died in his chair. Restful, considering.

"All clear" came the announcement from the remote overwatch loud and clear across their earpieces. The youngest soldier, Mini Riggs, visibly winced at the sound. It was a small movement, but his commander noticed. It was such a dramatic change from the practiced silence of a covert ops advance team.

"Relax soldier," Alex said after he saw the small head jerk.

Mini nodded and was ready for it when Overwatch spoke up again.

"Theta. Five targets, 30 yards ahead. Looks to be some sort of rest area. All five are asleep on cots."

"Copy that," Alex said. "Theta, let's move."

* *

Parts of the pyramid had been repurposed for habitation. Between the young, single members of Defenders of the Pure and a few high-ranking officials, they had created somewhat modest sleeping, eating and relaxation areas in the abandoned military facility.

This area, set up as a general sleeping quarters, housed a dozen or so military-grade cots. Five were currently occupied.

Theta heard them before they saw them. Snoring. Erratic patterns. Overlapping.

"Whoa," Granville said.

"I'm counting three distinct," Dave "Blue" Green said.

"With a room that loud, I wonder how many are wearing earplugs," Alex said over the throat mic system.

"No way to tell, Theta," Overwatch said. "I don't have that level of detail. Ice, be advised you have a third bogey coming toward the left bend."

"Copy that, Overwatch," came Ahab's voice over the team comm channel.

"Theta, you are clear to advance."

"Copy that, Overwatch," answered Alex. "Walnuts, Blue, take point. Blades. Mini and I will come in with suppressors. We'll try to do this as quietly as possible."

Alex and Mini pulled out their service pistols from back holsters. While there was not always weapon unanimity among the Wraith teams, both Alex Scott and Rick Everson liked to plan ahead.

All eight members of the team were carrying Berretta M9A3s. It was the pistol used by U.S. armed forces since the 1980s – a tried-and true design. The two men screwed the suppressors into place.

While many people can only rely on popular entertainment for weapon information, the silencer seen in movies simply doesn't exist. Film and TV would have people believe that a weapon equipped with a suppressor only makes a PUH sound when fired – like a cough or a loud whisper. A silencer might help, but the gun still sounds like a gun. The suppressor works to soften the transition of the superheated gases that escape a weapon's barrel when a shot is fired and reduce the noise of the pressurized explosion.

That said, the M9A3 was already comparatively quiet and a silenced gunshot would likely be absorbed into the environment before calling the rest of the Defenders to Alex's corridor.

Beef nodded to the rest of the team. They made it through the first three sleeping figures without a problem.

* *

The third soldier had fallen asleep holding a harmonica. As his left hand went slack, he dropped the small metal musical instrument and it clattered to the ground.

It wasn't a singularly loud noise, but in a sparse, concrete room, it echoed into the silence. The two remaining men awoke and were immediately shot in the face by Commander Alex Scott.

* *

Similarly-victorious, Team Ice met with Team Theta in what they determined to be the main storage room of the facility.

"I'm dark over here, Theta," Overwatch said over their team comms. "The camera system in this room is down or has been disabled. According to intel, this was the last known location of the target."

"Copy that," Ahab said and looked at Beef Scott. "I'm assuming there are 20 tangos in that room."

"Probably safe," Beef said. He was calling up the main blueprints on his wrist monitor. He scanned all around the line-drawings for 45 seconds before shaking his head. "It's about 80 by 80. Couple ventilation ducts. But only this door."

He indicated the door about 20 yards down the hallway from the two teams. There were giant double doors standing open that led into the room.

"It looks like this is a secondary storage," Alex continued. "For internal use. There was a primary outer storage with external access. Things like truck deliveries. It's been walled off from the outside."

Commander Everson nodded.

"I'm guessing that our target is in there because they never figured out what it was," he said.

"How do we know they never figured it out?" Dave "Blue" Green asked.

"Because this battle would be going a hell of a lot different, soldier," Beef said.

* *

Due to the easy-to-protect features of the room, the Defenders of the Pure had decided to congregate here. When communication with their sentries went down, leadership anticipated they were under attack. Because all four sentries were lost at almost the same time – nearly a mile apart – they assumed it was a coordinated, professional effort.

Now was the time for their last stand.

There were 30 soldiers taking up defensive positions all around the huge storage room. They were wielding various degrees of weaponry from single-shot hunting rifles to AR-15 assault rifles. Their training was just as varied as their gear.

The eight Wraith men stood stacked up at the door in single file. The challenge would be getting in through the bottleneck. Granville rolled in a small ball, covered in rubber. A piece of tech stolen from Allied Genetics – a small camera. The ball stopped about 10 feet into the storage room and activated. It began broadcasting a video signal back to the team's gauntlet computers.

"Okay, we toss in a couple flash-bangs. Ice will go in first and take positions on the left, Theta will take the right. Nice and easy." Ahab was speaking and looking at the video screen.

They started to hear gunfire from inside the room. Apparently, someone had noticed the little ball and was trying to take it out. There were perhaps a dozen shots and the camera feed stayed live. These men were poor shots, or, possibly, too amped up on adrenaline.

"That's encouraging," Beef said.

Suddenly, the firing stopped. The camera continued to broadcast.

"Okay," Ahab said. "While they're reloading and getting their wits. Let's go."

"Weapons free," Scott said.

Two men, Duncan "Glaze" Turner and Jimmie "Walnuts" Granville, each pulled a flash-bang grenade out of their combat webbing. It was an assault tool designed to both blind and deafen their opponents. It was a grenade without the shrapnel – a huge explosion of light and amplified sound. They threw their grenades only seconds apart and into different areas of the room to shock any soldiers who might be looking in different directions.

The result was instantaneous.

"Go," shouted Ahab. Immediately, his team ran into the room and found cover. Right behind them, Beef's team came in and scattered to the right. The lights in the room were on, but low. Only about 20 percent of the overhead lighting was still working. The room was large enough to have two levels. There was a set of stairs on the right that led up and around the back of the storage area to the office. It was basically a room within a room – elevated, with the front covered in glass.

Beef spotted a shooter positioned up there.

"Sniper up top," he said. "Glaze. Hit it with the boom."

While half of the team laid down cover fire, Glaze pulled his M32 grenade launcher off his back and aimed it at the elevated room. There was a loud THUMP sound and a long contrail of smoke as the grenade arced up and into the office. It was quickly followed by two more shots.

It seemed like all 30 DOTP men took cover at the same time.

WHAM WHAM WHAM

The three explosions occurred within seconds and the result was spectacular. The elevated office simply ceased to be. Soldiers who were beneath the structure were rained upon by debris. Bits of wood, glass and brick erupted all around the room.

The rest of the battle went even worse for the DOTP.

There were actually four men in the office – two snipers and their two leaders. As the men on the floor realized what had happened, the panic gripped different soldiers in different ways.

Five men immediately ran forward firing wildly at the Wraith soldiers. They were taken down by controlled fire.

After the five men who had broken ranks were gunned down by the assault force, the rest of the DOTP soldiers wondered what to do. In a matter of seconds, their snipers, their on-site leadership and five of their baddest men were gone.

They began firing at the Wraiths in an undisciplined manner – emptying their clips without once aiming, standing while reloading, changing cover without waiting for cover-fire. It was a madhouse. The two Wraith teams made easy work of them as their commanders stayed in control and called out orders – coordinating movement.

The final two surviving DOTP soldiers realized what had happened and threw down their weapons. The Wraiths ceased fire. It was Ahab who broke the silence over the team comms.

"We're not equipped to take prisoners," he said, calmly, the command buried in his statement.

The final two DOTP soldiers were killed on the spot.

* *

Timothy Jeremy Jackson.

The remote overwatch had continued to update their internal files on the Defenders of the Pure members who would likely be at the facility. They were a relatively small group with limited resources. For some reason, they had not risen in popularity as a militia like their parent organization, Clarke's Boys. The building's surveillance cameras weren't providing a clear enough picture to actually feed into facial recognition software, but the Wraith units' bodycams were more than enough.

Overwatch had been crossing members of DOTP off a DMV-enabled spreadsheet since the first minute of the assault. While there were still a few dozen members of the group unaccounted for, there were only about 10 left in the building that they could see.

And the remaining leadership figure was Timothy Jeremy Jackson.

He was more insightful than intelligent, but his ability to read a room was exceptional. Mr. Jackson was instrumental in the DOTP splinter group. By all accounts, Overwatch believed he was somewhere in the Nekoma Pyramid at this moment.

* *

"Wuddaya mean it's not here?"

Both Wraith teams had searched the large storage facility after the battle. They all had the image of the wooden crate with the part number stenciled on it. The two commanders even had descriptions of the actual unit in the event that the DOTP had opened the crate. Unfortunately, there was nothing here.

"Negative on the storage room?" asked Overwatch.

"Affirmative," Ahab said. "We're Oscar-Mike."

"Copy that," and Overwatch clicked off.

Theta and Ice had each taken a moment to reload and check their weapons in the big room. They didn't search the bodies or the other boxes in the warehouse area since they were after no intel other than asset relocation. They had left one man at the huge door.

"Well, if there's anyone else in the building," Beef said, "they certainly know we're here now."

Ahab nodded.

"Your element of surprise has evaporated, soldier," he said, smiling. "Now all you have left is my fearsome reputation."

"You want to send them an email?" Beef said, smiling. "You know. To trumpet your arrival?"

"I'll send *you* an email," Ahab said.

"Good one," Beef replied, clapping his fellow commander on the shoulder. "We're moving out."

* *

In his mind, it was thunderous applause. A stadium filled with jubilant supporters. In reality, it was eight kids in mis-matched uniforms looking at him with wide, terrified eyes. Sweating. One in the back was picking his nose when he thought no one was looking. Another was trying desperately to send a text, but the signal strength was unkind. They were under six floors of concrete and hard North Dakota soil.

Timothy Jeremy Jackson was attempting to rouse his troops for a final victory.

There was no escaping this scenario. The spotty surveillance footage showed a force of highly trained mercenaries rampaging through the facility overrunning their defensive positions. While they didn't have great coverage in the storage room, the explosions and gunfire told a story all their own.

Jackson collected the rest of his men in Sub-Control 1 – as it was stenciled on the outer door – and waited for their final encounter.

"The path we have chosen for the present is full of hazards, as all paths are," Jackson said to his troops. He was standing at the back of the room, furthest from the door, nearest the bank of primitive computer consoles. "But it is one most consistent with our character and courage as a nation and our commitments around the world. The cost of freedom is always high, but the Defenders of the Pure have always paid for it. And one path we shall never choose, and that is the path of surrender or submission."

"Is that JFK?" one young trooper said, listening, but watching the door for invaders. "He totally stole a JFK speech."

The man next to him nodded and bent into a crouch behind a stack of A4 paper storage boxes.

"What a schmuck," the first man continued, nodding next to the other man. "See you on the flip side, James."

"Our goal is not the victory of might," Jackson continued, "but the vindication of right. Not peace at the expense of freedom, but both peace *and* freedom."

Boom.

The men in the room had just barely recognized the chaff grenade that was tossed into the room. It exploded a sphere of rubberized particles that jammed the firing mechanisms of their weapons. The eight Wraiths, black and silent, stormed into the room holding their foot-long KA-BAR combat knives at the ready. They sliced their way through the enemy combatants with ruthless efficiency.

It was over before it started. The enemy leader had been more worried about delivering a rousing speech than taking up a defensive position – or even holding a weapon. He died unceremoniously, convulsing on the floor atop a spreading pool of blood – looking at his gaping chest wound.

"Easy money," Ahab said.

"And there we go," Beef said, nodding toward the corner.

"Sir, we have it," Walnuts said.

He was standing next to a wooden crate. Stenciled on the side was the United States flag and the stencil USAF-3213-77. It matched their mission objective. They didn't even need to open the box.

"Load it up, and exfil," Overwatch said. "It looks like we're getting new orders."

CHAPTER FOUR

THEY HAD ALL FAILED

THEY HAD COLLECTED in the main commissary of Facility Four to discuss what had happened over a heaping, hot plate of rations. "Astronaut food," as the team called it, had been generously stocked in the four pantries of Hell Island. After four months of living off the pre-packaged, just-add-water meals, the researchers had yet to make a dent in their supplies. Hell Island had been stocked to house hundreds of workers for several months between re-supply caravans.

The three of them sat at one table, green plastic plates in front of them, a decanter of reclaimed water in the center of the table. The distress beacon, ED-C10, sat quietly on a table in the corner – one of the six unoccupied seating areas.

"I'm not sure I ever saw that," Nick Jennings said. He spooned a mouthful of mashed potatoes off his plate with the utensil in his right hand and rubbed the stubble across his head with his left. Angered at his part in the death of Art, he shaved his head – from the neck up, everything but the eyebrows – with a maniacal energy. He had left his beard and head-hair in his bathroom sink and took a nap. Now, three hours later, the team was decompressing, having dinner.

"What's that?" Anna asked.

"Predator-on-predator crime," Nick said. "Like, I've never seen a documentary about sharks hunting other sharks. I always just assumed it was some sort of professional courtesy. But the way those dinos went after each other, I'll have to re-think the entire thing."

Everyone was silent around the table. They had put on some quiet jazz in the background to fill the ambiance. No lyrics, just music. They knew the risks when they signed up to work at Objekt 221 – even more so when Allied Genetics began developing excursion teams – individuals with a mixture of experience and knowledge. They were keen to recall warnings from every training session about indigenous lifeforms, fauna and even the atmosphere. They had even lost team members before – but this one struck too close to home. Since being abandoned four months ago, the team had fought hard to remain survivors until a rescue team would be sent.

Swallowing a forkful of shredded, freeze-dried roast beef substitute, Davis Brighton cleared his throat.

"There is no professional courtesy," he said. "It's more like the conservation of energy. Predators make it a habit to hunt weaker prey because it's easier. Imagine a lion hunting another lion. Evenly matched. The winner would expend more energy than would be recovered through eating his food. If something like that *did* happen, it would be more likely an interloper who came upon an injured or sleeping lion. Something like that. Some sort of extraneous variable."

He shrugged and went back to his food.

"I'm not sure *what* we witnessed."

Nick paused for a moment and drove his remaining food around the plate with his plastic fork.

"I saw a documentary with killer whales eating great white sharks," Nick said. "That's really the closest I ever got."

Anna nodded.

"I saw that, too," she said. "Maybe even the same documentary. Orcas are genius hunters and also jerks. It's been reported on numerous occasions when great whites clear out of a location, it's generally because the orcas have moved in. Nobody wants any part of them."

* *

"I suppose we just leave it here," Davis said.

They had finished their dinner about an hour ago and the three researchers had convened in the waiting area just outside the main control room. While its originally intended purpose had been lost, it was a large room just outside the facility's main control center. Ten days into their stay, the team started moving furniture around in an effort to make the living space theirs. They had moved several couches and chairs from storage to create a relaxing lounge area.

It was in this area that everyone now sat.

Nick, freshly shorn, was wearing jeans and a t-shirt that said "No Pressure/No Diamonds" across the back. Anna was wearing a light-blue company jumpsuit. Davis reclined in a corner chair wearing a pair of cargo pants and the black polo shirt he had initially worn on this excursion. They had found a few boxes of personal effects and suitcases with clothing at the facility, ostensibly, delivered in advance of the team who were going to rotate in. Clearly, that group of people were never going to show, so Davis and his team took ownership of all they saw. They figured that everything could be sorted out and apologies given when they were finally rescued. It was the very definition of "Easier to ask forgiveness than to seek permission."

"From what I can tell," Anna replied, "it's giving off a burst every few minutes. A discharge that includes coordinates. We can only hope that it's being picked up at O221."

"It makes sense to leave it in one place, then," Nick said, absently rubbing the stubble on the top of his head. "It makes sense to leave it static so we're easier to find."

Nods were shared all around the room and they sat in silence for nearly five minutes. Finally, it was Anna who spoke up.

"Are we just going to leave him there?"

"Not to sound disrespectful," Davis said, "I don't think there'll be anything left of him out there to bring back. I think we should have a quiet memorial service, though."

Nick Jennings nodded his head.

"Right on both counts. Whatever's left of him, I'm not sure any of us want to see."

"Yeah," Anna said, and then turned away from the rest of the team. "I suppose."

Everyone felt responsible. It was Anna's mission to run. Nick's facial hair caused the fault in his mask, slowing everyone down. Davis was stationed in mission control to alert the team and help them avoid danger. They had all failed. They had all gotten Arlington Beech killed.

"Yeah," Davis responded.

CHAPTER FIVE

LIKE A DONUT

"IT TOOK SOME time, but we were able to uncover some info about additional facilities." Angus Pope stood at the head of the big auditorium that occupied the north end of the capital K-shaped layout of the Anvil Canyon facility – generally referred to by the name given to it by the Soviet military during its Cold War construction, Objekt 221. They had amassed the military force – paid a heavy price plus insurance to Sergott Solutions – and selected the scientists from Precision Robotics that would take a trip to Ancient Crimea to track down the distress beacon.

The auditorium could seat more than 200 people. The seating arena was sloped down in the traditional fashion, all pointing toward the podium at the bottom center. The back wall was lined with huge monitors. Right now, they were cycling through various blueprints that had hand-written notations on them.

Angus paused in speaking and also paused the presentation going on behind him. The image froze and had a heading of **Facility Four**.

Everyone in the room had been given a briefing packet. Many were taking notes. All had turned to the page in their binders that featured the same blueprint that was on the screen.

Damon Butcher and Cadey Park both sat in the front row. They were two researchers who had been to Ancient Crimea, to "the other side" as many people called it, through Objekt 221's time portal. They both now worked for Precision Robotics thus were easy to coerce. Precision's leadership was having trouble convincing other former Allied Genetics employees to skip back in time after the Building 5 debacle just less than four months ago.

Damon and Cadey were joined in the front row by two of the military commanders – Alex "Beef" Scott and Rick "Ahab" Everson. They never explained their callsigns, and would command 15 soldiers into the distant past to both rescue the lost individuals and collect any data they might be able to.

Damon scribbled a note across the top of the Facility Four page. Hell.

Island.

"We were able to track the transponder beacon to these coordinates," Angus continued as he flipped back one page on his presentation and highlighted a section with a laser-pointer. It was a map of Ancient Crimea. Old school cartography. It was hand-drawn. He was circling a section of the map with the pointer. It was a small peninsula jutting into what was labeled as the Black Sea. "Matching those coordinates with maps of the area and other internal documents, we find the coordinates to pair with what is called Facility Four."

Finally, he switched back to the blueprint of the facility and then hit "slideshow" again on his laptop. There were eight or 10 artist renditions of the facility plus elevations and engineer notations about a section of the peninsula that needed to be removed. "The Moat."

"As you can see, Facility Four is circular in shape. Like a donut, but, you know, without the giant hole in the middle."

"So, like a hamburger bun," Damon said.

"Okay," Angus said. "Sure. I was thinking more along the lines of pastry, but I get it."

"Like an éclair?" Alex Scott offered.

"I think those are more tubular," Angus said. "We're more round here." He ran the laser-pointer in a circle around the perimeter of the facility on one of the drawings. "In any event, the structure is four floors, broken up into functional areas as you can see in your handout. Facility Four is ringed with what amounts to indestructible windows on two of the four floors. It is a research and observation facility."

He paused for a moment as his audience flipped through their binders, thick with data.

"In most documents, the facility was given a nickname," he continued. "Hell Island. Apparently, they were doing some genetic research, gene mods, hybrids, mutes. All kinds of fun stuff. Many of the experiments died on the table, but a few were released into the wild to chart the effectiveness of the changes. Air, land and sea-based. The research is spotty, but there's some pretty scary stuff."

"You're kidding," Ahab said, reading off one of the pages in his binder. "They had a dinosaur that stood on hind legs and had four arms? Some sort of super-predator?"

Angus nodded.

"Yeah. We're going to go through all of this together so you're well prepared. But a lot of it is not pretty. Let's move on."

* *

The presentation went on for another two hours and then there was a two-hour break for lunch and prep before the second half began. The excursion was going to be a strange hybrid of "hastily put together" and "planned to the smallest detail." Angus had no illusions about how long the three individuals in the snapshot might survive in Ancient Crimea. In truth, he didn't even know how long they had been there. The data on various excursion teams and their movements was frustrating – hyper detailed in some places, vague – or even missing – in others. It was obvious that Allied had been hiding things or, at the very least, compartmentalizing knowledge about their true organizational movements. The rescue of the missing team could answer numerous questions about Allied's research into that time period.

Many of those who had attended the earlier presentation were now in C-Wing's main cafeteria. With a skeleton crew operating the facility, Precision had strategically positioned their resources. Damon and Cadey were eating at one table. There were various other workers from other teams scattered around the large room. The two military commanders were eating quickly and had a stack of prep forms to go through. Angus had told them he wanted a list of the weaponry to take back to the Cretaceous.

Beef answered "All of it." Angus wanted a more accurate list.

The two men had promised to go over the on-hand list and prioritize it into five groups. They grumbled and took several binders with them. Right now, they seemed to be plowing through a lunch of egg-salad sandwiches.

"You were in the military, right?" Cadey asked.

"Yup," Damon answered around his own lunch – a chicken and pasta dish. He had carefully moved all of the broccoli florets to the side of the plate so they wouldn't contaminate the rest of his food.

"What's the deal with the nicknames? Beef? Ahab? I'm sure they all have them." She paused for a second. "Did you have one?"

"Sure, yeah," Damon said. "They're called callsigns, though, not nicknames, although they probably represent the same thing. As for how they started, I'm not sure."

Damon pushed the broccoli around just a bit. Punishing it for existing.

"I think it was rooted in a secrecy thing, right?" He almost asked it as a question to both himself and Cadey. "Like, if you were going to bomb Moscow, you couldn't say Operation Bomb Moscow. It had to be Operation Flaming Condor or something. I think commanders of operations were likewise given callsigns to add to the secrecy. Regular guys like me, it's probably more of a bonding thing than anything else."

"So, it's a nickname."

"I suppose so," Damon smiled. "But it's a military nickname, so it's clearly more substantial."

"What about *those* guys? Beef and Ahab? Does it have something to do with their history or mission experience?"

"Nah," Damon shook his head. "They usually have something to do with something embarrassing. We actually had a guy in my unit called Ahab. He only liked, um, bigger gals. If you get my meaning."

Cadey was silent for a moment and then the corners of her mouth turned downward.

"That's horrible," she said.

"Somehow you thought guys were all made up of sweetness and light?" Damon said. "You can think of a dirty euphemism for every nickname – military or not."

Cadey sighed and nodded.

"I suppose. I had a friend at uni that we called Berries. I won't even tell you where it came from."

Damon stood with his empty-ish plate and Cadey followed.

"Oh, come on. You *have* to tell me now."

"Maybe after the mission," she said, smiling.

"Deal."

* *

When they returned to the conference hall, Angus was standing at the podium with a lady. She was tall and held an easy smile. Even with a generally unassuming outfit, she carried herself with an unmistakable confidence. Powerful physically and mentally. She wore a flower print dress and had her long blonde hair pulled back into a ponytail. She was roughly the same age as Angus.

"This is AJ Fontana, on loan to us from Precision Robotics corporate in New York," Angus began as he addressed the group who were getting settled after their break.

For her part, AJ wore a polite smile and waved to the team.

"Hello everyone," she said. "Officially, my title is Team Lead, Management of Information Services and Operations. It's a bit of a mouthful, so I'm perfectly happy to reply to AJ. I'll be working here at O221 with Angus while you all are in the field. We'll be doing data mining in an effort to uncover anything that might be of use."

"But, how does that help, ma'am?" Alex Scott said, raising his hand at the same time he was speaking. "If you find something out, you can't tell us about it. Right?"

She nodded.

"Yes, outside of the hyper-technical mumbo jumbo of time travel, graviton spires and light-well wormholes, there is a communication deficiency. We are encouraged about the signal that the distress beacon is sending and Angus has uncovered some interesting research that Allied was doing before, well, *before*."

Angus had brought two chairs to the stage, away from the podium, and he and AJ sat down, facing the assembly. Angus still had the remote that controlled the presentation and his newly-introduced counterpart held a sheaf of papers.

"Okay," Angus said. "First order of business. Time travel."

CHAPTER SIX

KING OF THE DINOSAURS

THE TEAM WAS so large they had to come over in three waves. The first wave had the primary team members as well as the bulk of the essential equipment. Damon and Cadey stood next to Alex Scott and Rick Everson. There were two metal containers – one with weapons and one with provisions such as food and medical supplies – lining the back of the large area.

Damon remembered his trips into Ancient Crimea with a mixture of nostalgia and terror. Unknown technology. Unknown environment. Unknown hostiles. His first time, he very nearly had a panic attack both standing on the huge stainless-steel tiled octagonal shape they referred to as the 'launching pad' and arriving at the replica mission control room 100 million years in the past. Surrounded by a series of metal towers, he had watched the countdown on the huge display screen directly in front of them. And, then …

White.

A super-heated blast of sound, if that was possible.

And a popping sensation in his ears that, somehow, came from deep inside his brain. He had always thought of the sound as being reminiscent of someone thumping their thumb on the side of a heavy cardboard box that was only half filled with …. something. It was that same, almost hollow, sound.

As the world came into focus, he looked first to Cadey who was standing perfectly still with her hands up, palms together, fingers pointing toward her chin – a "flat" position as it was referred to in many Asian religions – with her eyes closed.

He then looked to Alex and Rick. They were also standing perfectly still, but they were looking straight ahead. Eyes up. Eyes wide. Not in shock or surprise. It was more of an aggressive alertness. Possibly, it came from military training. They were accustomed to arriving in hostile situations and making themselves hyper aware of danger.

When the light finally returned to normal, they found themselves standing in an exact replica of the room they left in Objekt 221. Only, in the Cretaceous.

* *

"What was that?" Anna asked the room in general.

They were all collected in the main control room of Hell Island, running various projects. It was as if all 6 computers in the room flickered on at the same time. Additionally, the main two screens imbedded in the control room's windows – a pale-blue HUD – activated. Foot-tall lettering scrolled across the bottom of the window screens as well as the computer screens in the room.

ACCEPTING OPERATIONAL UPDATES

With a rapidly filling status bar beneath it. The entire thing lasted no more than 15 seconds. The window HUD went back to a dormant state. The computers that had been previously turned off, turned themselves back off. The computers that had been quietly spinning away in sleep mode, went back to sleep.

"What the -?" Nick said.

* *

Finally, all three teams from Objekt 221 had arrived in Gamma Complex – the main launching pad in Ancient Crimea. It was a mirror-image in both structure and geographical position to O221 – connected by what was essentially a wormhole that erased 100 million years of history.

If, somehow, they could just stand in this same position for 100 million years, they would watch the Crimean military facility be built all around them.

The team consisted of 15 Wraith soldiers hired from Sergott Solutions with their two commanders and two researchers with Cadey Park and Damon Butcher leading the charge. Cadey and Damon were the last two scientists to make the Cretaceous excursion. They were 21-strong with a large range of weapons and tactical planning experience.

Cadey wasn't convinced of their odds for success, but, if there were people trapped here, she owed it to them to try to get them back to civilization.

"Check the gear and stack it up by the door," Beef said, commanding the group of troops. "We'll secure the transportation and line them up outside."

Everyone was dressed almost exactly the same. They all had on the dark green camo-style excursion suits. The protective gear was loaded with pockets and clips as well as a large backpack. The soldiers carried an impressive array of weapons. The scientists also carried weapons, but carried many defensive and health-centric pieces. For quick identification, they had versions of red and blue paint splotches across the tops of their faceplates. The soldiers all had red, while the two commanders both had orange. The scientists all had blue, while Cadey and Damon had a very pale teal.

Angus tried to explain that the faceplate HUD would automatically identify who they were looking at – "Like playing a videogame," he said – but the Wraiths figured a visual representation would help, too.

Damon knew they were giving themselves a way to measure casualties on the battlefield, but he chose to remain silent.

There were six metal crates, a combination of weapons and provisions, that the soldiers started going through. The two commanders pointed Damon at the door.

"Let's go," Ahab said. "Butcher, you're with us."

* *

"Crap on a cracker," Ahab said.

The three men had gone through the two massive steel doors that book-ended the decompression and purification chamber that separated Gamma Complex from the Cretaceous. They were immediately struck by the perceptive differences. For one, even though their suits were climate-controlled, the air was noticeably warmer. In fact, there was a small corner in the upper right of the faceplate HUD that listed both Internal and Ambient Temperature. They could see the Ambient Temperature rising steadily past 100 degrees Fahrenheit.

"I was only here a couple of times – a few hours each – and I never got used to it," Damon said.

They all three stood in place and just looked around. Several yards away from the corner of the building, they could see evidence of battles past. A large pile of bones – and a huge rib-cage – littering a section of the grass.

The faceplate had calculated local time to be right around 4 in the afternoon. The sunlight had a strange orange hue and many of the larger plants were covered in a hazy mist near their tops.

"There's a higher concentration of water in the atmosphere," Damon said, pointing to a clump of trees about 30 yards away, that looked like it was growing into a cloud – but it was simply a thick layer of mist. "It's like being in Miami. Thick, dewy air. Problem is that there's a much higher level of oxygen in the air. Lethal. The faceplate will protect you from it, just don't take it off."

Instinctively, the two soldiers ran the tips of the gloved fingers along the thick layer of foam that sealed the acrylic mask around their faces.

"Copy that," Beef said.

"Crap on a cracker," Ahab said again.

* *

"Whoa," Damon said as the huge door slid open.

Comparing the inside to the outside, Gamma Complex looked to be twice as big as it should have been. Essentially, the building was split in half. The front side represented scientific research and the back side represented Allied's private military. It was a simple visual illusion that prevented those coming in from the "science side" to even know there was a "military side." There was a brick wall jutting out about eight feet, perpendicular to the exterior of Gamma. This wall was intentionally overgrown with foliage and completely blocked the back half of the building from the casual observer. In truth, no one from the science side had ever wanted to explore around the perimeter of the building ... they had all wanted, every time, to immediately begin exploring the strange land that lay in front of them, not behind.

There was a separate launching pad inside that was still operational within an acceptable standard deviation. Just past that, was a large garage. It could be sealed and pressurized to work on various vehicles, but it was also built to stand open against the Cretaceous environment. There were spaces for several additional vehicles, but, right now, the room was populated by two Light Strike Vehicles (LSVs) – which were essentially armored dune buggies – and three enormous Joint Light Tactical Vehicles (JLTVs). These are what had elicited Damon's response.

"Yeah," Beef responded.

Manufactured by Oshkosh Defense, the JLTVs were the winners of a competition to become the military's replacement for the High Mobility Multipurpose Wheeled Vehicle (HMMWV) ... generally known as the HUMVEE. Parked in the Gamma Complex garage were three of these armored vehicles that, when standing side-by-side with a Humvee, looked like the original vehicle's bigger, angrier brother. It didn't help that they were painted a matte orange.

"Looks like they're the payload variation," Ahab said. Beef nodded, and stepped into the huge room. "Armored up. Enclosed bed. No offensive weapons. Doesn't exactly blend in, though."

"It's something to do with the dino's perception," Damon said. "I read about it. A blurb. In Angus's prep."

"Oh, yeah," Alex "Beef" Scott nodded. "Sure. Me too."

"What? They can't see 'em?" Rick "Ahab" Everson said. Beef looked at him. "No. Fine. I didn't read the whole binder."

"Not invisible. Not really," Damon said. "It's more like they see it and dismiss it. Something about that color in particular makes them think the vehicle is more like a huge flower. Completely non-threatening. As long as we don't do anything aggressive like run into them or fire weapons from the vehicle, we should be virtually, yeah, invisible."

The three men each walked to their own vehicle, got in, and fired them up. They drove out of the garage, closed the door, and lined the JLTVs across the front of the building – by the main Gamma Complex door.

"Glaze, we're here," Ahab said into his faceplate's mic. On the HUD, an image of Duncan "Glaze" Turner popped up. In fact, all 20 people could hear what Ahab was saying. "Start bringing out the crates."

"Copy that, sir," Glaze said over the faceplate speakers. "Wraiths. Load up. Oscar Mike."

* *

"Did you see that?" one of the soldiers said as he stood near the front passenger tire of the center JLTV. They had loaded the metal crates into the vehicles and were about to get in. Cadey was reminding everyone that, while the vehicles were sealed against the environment, they were going to keep their faceplates on during the ride.

The soldier was pointing at the ground, to the right, toward the corner of the Gamma Complex building. They had let various clumps of trees and shrubbery grow around the building when it wouldn't hinder the windows or doors.

"Whatcha got, DuPree?" Ahab asked.

"It was a – uh – I don't know," DuPree said. His HUD was spooling through several images trying to capture a quality look and link it up with the mission database. "Looked like a big centipede. Ran into those bushes." He indicated the heavy shrubs at the corner of the building.

DuPree took one step forward of the center JLTV, toward the clump of bushes, and all hell broke loose.

* *

It looked like a centipede, but it was nearly two feet long and just more than eight inches thick across its body. Its main color was black, but it had very bright orange legs and an orange diamond pattern running down the length of its back.

All 21 faceplates were running through the same decision tree as the central computer attempted to identify this creature. The HUD pulled an image and slotted it to the side of the screen. It was given the title STONE CENTIPEDE (?ERMAC?) while additional text scrolled by underneath.

It ran directly at DuPree and wound itself around his right leg. Its fangs were visible as it tried to bite through the protective titanium-weave and carbon-fiber plating on his thigh.

"Get it off, get it off," shouted the soldier as he stumbled backward. He tripped against his own feet and fell to the ground near the front tires of the huge military vehicle. Soon, he was swarmed by 12 more of the giant, angry insects. DuPree pulled his KA-BAR combat knife out of a thigh holster and began slashing at the centipedes. He caught one right across the body and it fell and twirled off his torso, leaking a gelatinous green liquid. The rest, sensing some sort of new danger, jumped away from the fallen soldier and stood on the hard-packed prairie grass in a semi-circle around DuPree who scrambled to his feet.

He held the knife at arm's length in his right hand and used his left hand to wipe a fistful of goop from the protective faceplate.

With this action accomplished, he grabbed the custom FN P90 submachine gun out of his left thigh holster. Outside of the modified trigger guard to account for the larger, heavier gloves, the heft of the weapon was spot-on.

"No, no, no," Beef shouted.

But it was too late.

DuPree pulled the trigger and raked a third of the clip in a wide curve right into the bodies of several of the stone centipedes. Four lay dead or dying in addition to the one he sliced open with his knife. The rest of the insects scattered back to their fortress inside the thick shrubbery. The soldier was breathing hard as the adrenaline began to burn off. He wasn't facing physical exertion – just mental.

Against the all-natural backdrop of sounds, the clatter of the SMG had sounded positively deafening. The group could hear various animals scattering, calling and roaring in response to the unnatural mechanical sounds.

There was one sound, though, that seemed to puncture all the others. It was a loud, high-pitched roar. It was a wheezing sound that was close, but also higher up than it should have been.

Damon and Cadey immediately looked at each other and said, simultaneously:

"T-Rex."

At the same time, all 21 HUDs crackled to life again.

WARNING! TYRANNOSAURS DETECTED!

"Plural?" Damon asked no one in particular. As if on cue, a second wheezing roar answered the first. The warning klaxons in the faceplates indicated they were about to be flanked.

"We need to get gone," Ahab said, holding his matching FN P90 at the ready. He had two heavier weapons strapped to his back, but he had grabbed the little black SMG almost on pure instinct.

Beef, however, saw the situation for what it was. A no-win situation. He processed all the factors in less than a quarter-second.

There were too many individuals to get into the vehicles or into Gamma Complex itself. They might be able to all get into the vehicle maintenance garage quickly enough. But that would leave the three JTLVs exposed. If the T-Rexes decided to nose around, they could easily overturn or destroy the monstrous vehicles. The building would be safe, but to a 30-foot-tall lump of muscle, the big cars would look like toys.

After another quarter-second he was starting to formulate a plan.

"Blue Paint. Start heading back to the garage. Hurry, now. Small access door's code is Christmas. 1225."

"Copy that," Damon said and took charge of leading the rest of the scientists back to the garage. He felt that with his experience, he would be a solid go-between for the soldiers and the researchers.

"Walnuts, auto-drone. We need to get eyes on these things."

"Copy that," replied Jimmie "Walnuts" Granville as he pulled a black drone out of his backpack. He activated it and flipped a switch that changed the color from black to bright blue – nearly matching the color of the sky. Using a remote, he sent the drone directly up in the air where it would hover autonomously. Walnuts clipped the remote control to his belt and the video feed started coming in to the faceplate HUDs.

"Rufus, Cheese, I need you in Vehicles A and B. Back 'em up and park 'em behind C, against the building. If the Rexes want to come down this path, we don't want to get 'em stepped on."

"Copy that," both men said and moved to the driver's doors of the two huge trucks.

"Forty seconds out, Commander," Walnuts said. "Moving cautiously."

"Got it," Beef said. "Weapons free. Heavies. Looks like we've already stirred up some trouble. Some kind of record for us."

"Hoorah," Ahab said.

* *

"Okay," Angus had said, and nodded to Damon. "First order of business. Time travel."

They had reconvened for the second term of the day's prep meeting. It was a robust itinerary, and Angus had jumped right in without any sort of preamble. Damon was now standing at the podium with Angus. He was the one person in the room who overlapped all three vectors at play – Precision Robotics, Allied Genetics and military training. Angus wanted to make sure to position him as an authority before sending this huge excursion back to collect the missing researchers and any data they might have gathered in the last four months.

"It's called a Sheffield Vortex," Damon said, addressing the fifty or so people in the auditorium. The excursion would be 21-strong, but many Precision employees were attending as they would also be providing on-site support. "A modified Sheffield Vortex. It's a sort of black hole but more accurately described as a *thin spot*. We believe there are 12 or 13 of these spots around the Earth – Vile Vortexes, they're called, including one in the Bermuda Triangle – but this is the only one that's been found, studied and exploited. It operates as sort of a portal to this exact place on Earth, but 100 million years ago."

There were some murmurs around the room. Some people were flipping pages in their thick mission briefing binders looking for the pages describing this phenomenon.

"Throughout Earth's history, there are local legends about ghost voices and paranormal activity – generally centered around areas of strong spirituality. Vortexes. They are natural conduits. Like a screen door. But, to Allied's credit, they were able to apply some bafflingly complex math and technology to actually, well, to *open* the door."

He paused for effect, before switching to the next frame of his presentation.

"And step through."

Behind him, on the giant screen, was a photograph – not a painting or computer graphics – of a triceratops, surrounded by trees and bushes with bright orange and red blooms.

"For better or worse."

He snapped to the next slide and it was a selfie – a researcher wearing full excursion gear, giving the thumbs-up, with the triceratops peacefully grazing on some prairie grasses behind him.

It brought a laugh from the room.

* *

"It's here," Walnuts said into his faceplate mic – a warning immediately broadcast to the other 20 faceplates as well as the central computer that recorded every interaction.

As soon as he spoke, the team both heard and saw the T-Rex. As his head peeked over the roof of Gamma Complex, he once again unleashed a high-pitched roar. The Wraith team had lined up near the trucks. They were playing a delicate game. They didn't want to expose the JLTVs, but they needed some sort of cover.

As indicated by the faceplate's HUD, this dino was above the average determined by modern paleontology at nearly 30-feet tall. He held position and his earlier call was answered.

"Second tango is hanging back," Walnuts said, examining the data feed from the drone. "Looks like they're on a reconnaissance mission."

"Copy," Beef said. "Let's see what he does."

The 17 soldiers were breathless watching the spectacle in front of them. They had watched Pope's briefing and saw both photos and video of the different dinosaurs. But seeing the king, live and in color, in his natural habitat, was awe-inspiring.

Much of what paleontology had guessed at was correct. He seemed a little taller yet somehow lither and more muscular than his portrayal in movies. The coloring was also darker – almost a brownish green. And the roar was completely different.

Otherwise – tyrannosaurus rex was shocking in his beauty and more than a little frightening.

Somehow, he seemed quicker than he should have been.

"I don't want to kill it," Beef said to the team. "I'd love to dissuade him from coming down here, if possible."

"Will a Parabellum pierce its hide?" Cheese asked, fresh from moving the heavy armor.

"No data," Ahab said.

Cheese took his pistol out of a thigh holster and sighted down the barrel.

"Put one into the ground by his feet," Beef said. "See if we can't change his mind."

Cheese immediately fired a single shot. It made a thump sound as the round embedded itself into the ground between the beast's feet. The Rex looked down at the hole in the ground and then directly at Cheese. It opened its mouth, displaying dozens and dozens of razor-sharp teeth. The team could see ragged bits of flesh stuck between its teeth and a couple smears of blood along the left side of its face – evidence of a recent battle. Clearly, he wasn't hungry, just curious.

"Uh oh," Beef said. "Fan out. Gun wall at the trees. Give me a couple more shots into the ground."

Wordlessly, the team followed their commander's instructions. They quickly moved across the alley between the lineup of JLTVs and the thick copse of trees. Cheese put five more rounds into the ground as they moved to keep the Rex at bay. True to form, he didn't move, but he watched the soldiers form up a new position to protect their flank and keep the action away from their only conveyances in Ancient Crimea.

Ten of the Wraith soldiers formed up a small defensive wall – five in a crouch, five in a standing firing stance. Ultimately, their goal was to turn invisible and hope the tyrannosaur decided to amble along on its original path – forgetting about the dead centipedes as well as the six shots fired at it. Ahab was calculating how far they would let the beast track them down the wide alley between the building and the trees before they had to start shooting to kill. For his part, Beef did a short manipulation with his fingers to move the drone video feed from his faceplate HUD to the wrist-mounted computer they all wore. He did this to free up some space in his vision.

Three seconds after he made this modification, the empty space in his HUD was taken up by a warning message. And then another. And then a third.

WARNING! TEAM MEMBER "SNOW DAY!" FLATLINE.

Followed by.

WARNING! TEAM MEMBER "SLICKS!" FLATLINE.

Followed by the more ominous –

WARNING! UC-0104 "GOLIATH" DETECTED!

"Oh no," Damon said over the faceplate speakers. "We're gonna need to get out of here."

WARNING! TEAM MEMBER "FEEDER!" FLATLINE.

It was something out of a horror movie. A 10-foot tall monster with two thick legs and four muscular arms all capped by impossibly sharp claws exploded out of the tree coverage between the Wraith gun wall and the still-cautious T-Rex.

It was the still-unclassified predator UC-0104. The central computer had given the species a nickname – Goliath – but had stayed with the alphanumeric classification as no official name had been entered. It was only discovered shortly before the war, in a literal sense, between mega companies Allied Genetics and Precision Robotics, that resulted in Precision taking ownership of the O221 outpost and, hence, the wormhole to the Cretaceous. Since no additional work had been completed by Allied's researchers, the beast remained unclassified.

The Goliath paused and looked from the T-Rex to the soldiers to the cars. What seemed like an eternity to the soldiers, passed in an instant. The T-Rex took a deep breath to roar for help of the other dino. In that moment, the Goliath took three bounding steps and launched itself back toward the thick copse of trees.

As he passed, though, he reached out his right two arms, claws fully extended, and raked them across the belly of the Rex. The giant dinosaur wasn't even sure what had happened at first. Just as suddenly, the Goliath had disappeared into the trees again. To a man, the soldiers had watched the UC dive back into the trees, presumably, to go about his business. They turned back to the T-Rex, who had taken a stumbling step backward. In excruciating slow motion, his wounds began to seep blood. He took another step and was almost clear of the front of the building and the front edge of the JLTV that had been designated as "C."

The blood-flow had increased and the skin in six long cuts across his stomach had started to expand. The T-Rex roared in pain.

"Advance," Ahab said. "Let's see if we can drop him in the pasture past Gamma."

He had pulled a vicious looking shotgun off his back and held it at the ready. It was an MPS AA-12, nicknamed the "Sledgehammer." It was an assault shotgun set to fire full auto. He had equipped it with a 32-shell drum magazine with two more strapped down his left leg. Another Wraith soldier, Hux, held his own version of the same weapon. The two men advanced side-by-side and fired at the dying T-Rex mercilessly.

Aided by a near-zero recoil, the Sledgehammers had amazing accuracy at that distance. Six shots from each of the two Wraiths had turned the T-Rex's body into a horror-show. The blood flow had turned into a waterfall, soaking the ground. He continued to stumble backward even as his lungs filled with blood. Finally, the Rex fell to his side and died, well past the path of the JLTVs and several yards into the clearing.

The men had already stopped firing and started to re-holster the auto-shotguns.

"King of the dinosaurs, my ass," Ahab said under his breath.

"Hoorah," replied Hux.

* *

"Let's load up the vehicles," Beef said as Walnuts landed the drone and began packing up. The other T-Rex had left and the Goliath wasn't being picked up on the faceplate sensors. They had decided to leave the three dead soldiers for now and get back on the move to locate the distress beacon. "Butcher, bring up the blue paint and take a look at DuPree's armor."

"Copy that," Butcher said, emerging from the garage section of the facility with Cadey and the rest of the O221 researchers in tow.

It became a 30-minute process to load all of their gear equally across the three JLTV trucks and then pack in each of the team members. They pulled a replacement faceplate from storage for

DuPree but, outside of a few surface scratches, his enviro-suit was perfectly fine.

With all the doors of Gamma Complex buttoned up, the team rolled out. Beef, Ahab and Damon drove the three JLTVs. The giant HUDs on the inside of each vehicle's windshield displayed a directional finder, a distance to target and a faint overlay of the best map Angus had been able to download into the mission computer. As soon as all three vehicles exited the Gamma alley and turned right into the large prairie, the convoy stopped. Beef had slammed on his brakes.

It was in response to the HUD warning.

WARNING! UC-0104 "GOLIATH" DETECTED!

"Not again," he muttered.

As suddenly as before, the Goliath had leapt from out of a jungle of trees slightly north of the Gamma building. They weren't sure if this was the same beast from earlier or part of a larger family that had taken up residence around the O221 wormhole.

With a sudden ferocity, the beast crouched and launched himself at the lead vehicle in one smooth, instant motion. He landed on the hood of Beef's JLTV and snarled at the inhabitants of the truck through the windshield.

He pulled back the upper right fist of his upper right arm and released a mighty roar. Just as he started to swing the fist in toward the supposedly unbreakable acrylic composite windscreen, the monster simply ...

Exploded.

One moment he was there, the next he was a smoking, unrecognizable meat pile.

"Holy cow," Beef said.

He looked down to the right of the steering column and pulled the lever for the windshield wipers. As the glass slowly cleared, blood-smear by excruciating blood-smear, they could see what caused the explosion.

Three people.

Dressed just like Beef's excursion team. The missing researchers. The image from Pope's decoded distress signal.

"Four down," Anna said, and holstered the grenade launcher across her back.

CHAPTER 7

BULLET SCARCITY

THE CONVOY OF military vehicles had traversed the five miles in a little more than 30 minutes. They kept their speed low in an effort not to attract any unwanted attention and had to stop once for a family of herbivores to cross their path. They had rumbled across the bridge that covered the peninsula's moat – more like a small river – and watched it rise back into the protective position after they passed.

Now, having parked in the massive underground garage, they were milling about a large conference room on the south edge of the curve of the building. They had a sweeping view of the water, the road down which they drove, and the trees beyond it. It was staggering in its beauty and simplicity.

"I never got used to it," Cadey said. She was standing in front of the window with Alex Scott. He stood with his arms crossed over the t-shirt he had worn under his enviro-suit. It was punctuated with sweat-marks, but he didn't bother to change. They were only going to be on Hell Island long enough for the missing researchers to collect their gear, their personal effects, and shut down all non-essential systems. He had a checklist from Angus.

He wore a jet-black t-shirt with the stylized skull-and-crossbones logo of the Wraiths with huge lettering stitched across his back: PROBLEM SOLVED.

"How many times have you been here?" Alex asked.

Cadey shook her head.

"Never to this facility," she said. "But I came on excursions about, oh, about a dozen times. You think you're going to get used to it. The lighting. The plants. The giant dinosaurs roaming the land. But you never do."

Alex nodded.

"I'm sure. Trying to do the detached military thing, but, in the back of my head, there's a little voice just screaming at me. *This is awesome!*"

He smiled and Cadey smiled back.

"Sure is," Cadey said.

Damon Butcher walked up holding a clipboard. The four team leads all had the printed checklist that Angus had devised.

"Hey," he said, and received a chorus of responses from Cadey and Alex. Rick Everson saw them congregating and came over. Ahab towered over everyone – nearly a foot and a half taller than Cadey – and his biceps were pushing the limits of his own Wraith t-shirt. It was heather gray with the logo in white covering his whole back.

"Hey," he said to the rest of them, and received the same chorus as Damon had.

"Moving right along," Damon said, reading off his notes. "Personal effects have been loaded into the JLTVs. There actually wasn't that much as most of the stuff they've been using was stuff left here when the place was being built. Brighton has finished downloading their mission journals and data sheets for transferal. They want to do a quick dinner – or whatever food is due at whatever time it is over here – and then head out. They've been eating extreme rations for the last several months and want to go out with style."

"We'll still need to reset the beacon," Alex said. "Wheels up in two hours?" Rick nodded in response.

"It's weird," Rick said. "I kinda wanna hang out and explore, but I also kinda wanna get home ASAFP."

"Right?" Cadey said. "I always expected to be stepped on by a dino while documenting a flower or something. I always felt like this place was going to kill me – even if by accident."

The four looked out the windows, quietly hoping they would experience a boring drive from Facility Four back to Gamma Complex – yet somehow certain that they weren't going to.

* *

"We knew something had happened," Nick Jennings said, pushing a fork of food into the corner of his mouth. "You see, the computers over here did an auto-update. We came to find out that it only happened when the rift was crossed. Essentially, you guys brought over the communication and system changes that we had been missing for four months."

"Huh," Cadey said. "Didn't realize that."

"Yeah," Anna said. "Same here. Because, as an excursion team, we were only ever on one side of it. As a group, we'd bring our own update here with us. No team had ever been left here for an extended period of time to notice things weren't communicating as intended."

"Yup," Nick said. "So, we geared up and headed over to Gamma to see what might have happened."

"And you torched a Goliath for us," Ahab said. "Thank you for that. Would have been a pain to stop the truck, get out, cut him in half, get back in … way too much work." He smiled as he sopped up some gravy with a piece of biscuit and tossed it into his mouth.

"No problem," Nick said, saluting.

"So, the entire purpose of your excursion is a rescue mission?" Davis Brighton asked. "You were sent back here to grab us and go back? Nothing more?"

Cadey shook her head.

"Those are our orders," she said. "Button up and head back. Oh, we need to reset the beacon."

Damon nodded in response.

"Great," Davis said. "I'm sure Allied'll be glad to have us back. Three MIAs to cross off the list."

The soldiers all became very interested in their food as Damon and Cadey shot each other a look. Davis noticed and hefted one eyebrow in a questioning manner.

"What?"

"Allied Genetics and Precision Robotics are corporate rivals. Mortal enemies," Damon said. "There was something of a net war starting just as you came over here. The stress was getting to the organization. In fact, my entire excursion was murdered and Cadey and I were put in a holding cell in O221. Probably to be shot and buried in an unmarked grave out back."

"Jesus," Anna said.

"Yeah," Cadey said and got quiet. "We'll need to look at the timeline. Just curious. I think you guys came over either right before or right after us. Probably right after because I don't remember hearing any sort of alerts. The reason no one came back and looked for you, was what Damon was leading up to." She waved at him as an indication that he was given the floor again.

"Right," Damon said, pushing his plate away. "Eventually, Precision sent these guys," he waved to indicate the Wraiths, "to rescue us and ultimately take over the O221 facility. A hostile corporate takeover."

"That's not how that works," Anna said.

Damon nodded.

"I know," he said. "There're some bizarre delicacies that are being worked out. I think the illegal nature of what Allied was doing is keeping them mum. There might also be some, um, blackmail going on. I'm staying out of the corporate stuff. Doing what I'm told. Collecting a paycheck."

Everyone was silent for a moment, taking in the oddity of what was heard. A hostile takeover wasn't necessarily meant to be physically hostile … with guns … there were laws against that, weren't there?

"I wanna go back for a minute," Nick said. "You mentioned *the Goliath*. Is that what they've named the UC-0104?"

Cadey shook her head.

"We've started giving the unclassified dinos nicknames, sort of, as a start to the classification process," she looked at Anna. "There's a lot of people trying to play catch-up. I'm sure you'll get the full debriefing when you get back."

"Or we'll be shot," Davis said.

"Not gonna happen, sir," Alex said. "We're to bring you back safe and sound. There's no insidious nature to our plan. Several former Allied employees wanted to leave O221 and were allowed to go. No mass grave out back, if you catch my meaning, sir."

"Honestly," Ahab piped in. "If they were just going to kill you, we'd have done it already."

Davis nodded, but remained skeptical.

"Okay," he said. "That makes sense. In a barbaric sort of way."

There was an uncomfortable moment of silence.

"Something's been nagging at me, and I finally just remembered what it was," Alex said. "After you exploded the dino, you said *four down*. Are you keeping score?"

Anna nodded, frowned for a moment and then smiled.

"Wanna see something cool?"

* *

The three missing researchers and the four excursion team leads went to a smaller room. It was along the same curved outer wall on the same floor, but it was more of a computer/tech room. There were several workstations, a server tower in the far corner and three large television monitors along the far wall. They had about a foot of blank wall space between each one.

Anna sat down at one workstation that was off-set – almost as if this was a boss or supervisor's chair. In a university computer lab, this space would be reserved, for example, for an instructor. She began typing against a keyboard that wasn't really there. It was a laser projection onto the table-top. Damon was looking at her, frowning.

"Cool, right?" she said, noticing.

"Haven't decided yet," Damon said. "So much of typing is about the tactile experience." He paused. "Plus, there have been studies linking the click-clack sound of a keyboard to something close to comfort."

Anna shrugged.

"They're not *all* set up to do this," she said. "But you get used to it. Cuts down on office supply costs. Okay, look up there."

She hit one final "key" and the three TV monitors silently slid together to form one large screen. It came to life with the Allied Genetics logo and was followed by some dense writing in a green font.

"It basically spells out the name, date and parameters of a study," Anna said as Damon, Cadey, Alex and Rick all stepped forward toward the now-monstrous screen. Davis and Nick were also in the room; they had seen this footage before. "It's something called an *interaction study* for what you would call UC-0104 … and eventually called The Goliath. The study's dated about five years ago."

The text faded into one more half-page of text.

"A lot of the files are locked," Nick said. "But a big part of what they were doing here was centered on genetic experiments. It's a hybrid with some mods thrown in. There are also some bizarrely human characteristics."

Davis was silently watching the screen, scowling.

Soon, the text faded once again and the image took up the three-screen combo. It was a wide shot of one of the vistas. It could have been the prairie that separated Gamma Complex from Facility Four … or it could have been a completely different area. Cadey, in a small part of her mind, was struck by how amateurish the video presentation was. Clearly, this information was put together in-house, but it didn't seem like much effort was put into it. Maybe they were rushed?

Text began to populate the left side of the image. Things like date, time, weather, and other critical factors lined up in bold type to indicate the start of the experiment. The vista shot itself began to slowly rotate through five cameras ... four drones and a stationary cage-cam. From one of the drone shots, they could see a version of the same JLTV they had driven, although this one was more like a pickup truck, with a four-person cab and an open rear bed. It was painted the same matte orange as they had already encountered. In the bed, though, was a huge cage with a huge reptilian monster in it.

Alex absently wondered where that particular vehicle had ended up. A lot can happen in five years, but the JLTVs are substantial vehicles and they hadn't seen that one at Gamma or any like it in the basement garage of Hell Island. Were there other facilities in this section of Ancient Crimea?

The video went back to the cage-cam. The Goliath was clearly agitated as the truck stopped. There was a new, sixth camera. It showed the interior of the driver cab of the JLTV. There were two heavily armored men in the front and two more in the back seats. The driver reached up to a ceiling-mounted control panel and pulled a silver lever. Back to the cage-cam and the image showed the hydraulic doors of the bed and cage open simultaneously.

Almost unconsciously, Cadey uttered "Uh oh."

The Goliath, tagged as EX-AP047 onscreen, launched himself out of the cage as if he was rocket-propelled. He landed nearly 20 feet away from the vehicle and stopped his momentum. He slowly turned his head, flexed his four arms and looked to be considering attacking the transportation. It was only for a brief moment as something else had caught his attention.

The scene switched to the extreme overhead shot provided by DRONE 1, as indicated on the image. It was approximately 100 feet above the action, enough to give it the wide shot that resembled a map. The truck remained motionless. Centered in the frame was the Goliath. Entering the frame from the bottom, East, as indicated by the digitally-inserted compass, was a tyrannosaurus rex. The drone HUD highlighted the two dinos and did a sweep with certain limitations imposed – it was looking for anything bigger than 3 feet. It noted the two dinos and the four soldiers. Nothing else.

"Here we go," Anna said from the control room. All seven people stood staring at the screen, unblinking, unbreathing.

The T-Rex came roaring, exploding out of the tree-line 30 yards from what would eventually be nicknamed the Goliath. The Goliath had already turned away from the JLTV with the cage in its truck-bed. He now followed the movements of the T-Rex with a steely gaze. Drones 2 and 3 were at ground level, but hovering about 100 yards away from the action, basically interspersing a side-view for the edited video.

With only a moment's hesitation, the T-Rex rushed toward the newcomer – seeing him as a threat to what was clearly the Rex's territory – and the Goliath matched his intensity. At 10-feet tall but nimble, EX-AP047 covered the 30 yards quickly. The Rex was more than twice the height of the interloper, but he clearly wasn't as fast. Perhaps, if he had gotten up to full speed on open terrain, he would win a footrace – but two beasts rushing together over 90 feet, the EX got up to max speed faster than the Rex ever would have dreamed.

The T-Rex roared and the Goliath responded outside of what anyone had expected – it dove for the ground and slid right between the Rex's legs. Aided by the moisture of the morning grass and the wide-set hips of the Rex, the EX glided along the ground and caught himself against the massive dinosaur's tail. He gripped the tail with two sets of clawed arms and began viciously attacking the tail with his teeth. In only a few seconds, the Goliath wrenched the final three feet of the T-Rex's tail right off and flung it aside.

It was anthropomorphic, but Damon could have sworn the beast smiled as he tossed the useless lump of flesh away.

The last three feet of the Rex's tail was poorly vascularized. He began to bleed immediately from the wound, but he was ultimately more enraged than in pain. The Goliath danced backward, clasping his claws open and closed, looking up at the T-Rex, who continued to roar.

With jaws open wide, the T-Rex feinted to the left and lunged at the Goliath to the right. The smaller dino, though, was ready for the move. Again, he danced backward and raked a set of claws against the Rex's cheek when he was at his lowest point. It was a glancing blow, but it left the deep green marbled skin across the right side of the Rex's face with three deep gashes that immediately started bleeding.

As the Rex backed up and stood to his full height and roared, the Goliath stood his ground and flicked the claws of his right hands.

"Did you see that?" asked Alex. "He just flicked the blood off his claws. I've never seen that sort of awareness in a predator locked in a fight."

There was silence around the computer lab.

"He's playing with him," Ahab said. "He's playing with the T-Rex." Ahab was staring at the screen intensely, as if trying to study a boxer's moves before an upcoming fight. He had a scowl on his face and his lips were pursed.

It was DRONE 3, now, that came in close to the action. The T-Rex lowered his huge head, nearly half the height of the Goliath in and of itself, and roared right in the smaller beast's face. He was not intimidated, and, if truth be told, almost seemed angry at this blatant disregard of his personal space. In a spin move that defied explanation, the Goliath lifted himself off the ground and raked six sets of claws – four arms and two legs – in turn across the throat of the T-Rex. Blood and gore immediately began flowing out of the big reptile. The image on the screen paused and rewound. It played again in super slow motion.

Damon looked back to see if Anna was doing it. She held up her hands, palms out.

"It's part of the presentation," she said.

Damon turned back to the screen to see the fourth, fifth and sixth appendages tear through the flesh of the King of the Dinosaurs like nothing. The Goliath landed gracefully having completed his spin and danced backward a few steps as the Rex slowly fell to lie prone on the ground.

While they had all been surprised by the entirety of the interaction, they weren't ready for what came next. The Goliath strolled the 20 yards into the jungle that lined the East side of this plains area. The image switched to the overhead drone. The Goliath was out of sight for only a few seconds. Suddenly he reappeared.

"Oh my God," Cadey said, her hands immediately covering her mouth. She had watched this entire video with a sort of detached scientific curiosity. She had seen one of these monsters up close – twice, including the attack just this morning. Now, though, she has horrified to realize, just as Ahab had said, the Goliath was simply toying with the Rex. He had never been in any danger at all.

The Goliath was dragging a huge fallen tree branch.

The branch was easily six feet long and as big around as a basketball. The Goliath dragged the piece of wood behind him over to the Rex.

"This is ridiculous," Damon said.

The Goliath swung the branch over and over like a baseball bat. He beat the T-Rex's head until it was nothing but a gory stain on the ground. He dropped the branch and then seemed to remember the truck. The camera from the cage in the JLTV showed the Goliath in shocking clarity as he ran straight for the big vehicle and then, blackness.

* *

"You *made* it to be like that?" Damon asked Anna, but the question was directed at all the researchers in the room.

"Well," Anna said, "*I* didn't make anything, but it looks like Allied had built this facility for genetic modification and training. Facility Four was fully operational for quite a while even though it was never totally completed. They must have been excited to start."

"Why was it abandoned?" Cadey asked.

Davis shrugged.

"We couldn't find any sort of directive about that," he said. "There were some personal effects. Clothing. Things that had either been left here or shipped here in advance of the next rotation. Personal files had been scrubbed."

"Do you know how many of those things were created?" Beef Scott asked.

"There were about a dozen hybrids being studied," Davis said. "A few different versions of, um, the Goliath. We've just come to call them 47s. That was the designation of the science experiment. Apex Predator #47."

"How many are still in the wild?"

Anna shrugged.

"We've been cataloging them," she said. "It was hard to get an accurate number from the science computers. Either they were intentionally scrubbed or," she paused, "well, that's probably it. I wouldn't expect such shoddy record-keeping. Something was buried in the files." She paused for a moment. "We've killed four. They had originally released 12. That we know of. There could be as many as 20."

"Jesus."

"We're killing them as we go," Davis said. "Because we're afraid those things are vicious enough and could upset the balance of evolution."

* *

They were reaching the end of their checklist and many of the excursion team had collected near the command center. Nick grabbed the distress beacon and walked it over to a small workstation. He put it on the desk and stepped away.

"We couldn't go out and hunt them, per se, because of bullet scarcity," Nick said.

"Bullet scarcity?" Damon asked.

"Yeah," he answered. "We were pretty well stocked out here, but as the days and weeks went by, we were starting to believe that no one would come back. Applying Occam's Razor, we figured there was some sort of technical issue on the O221 end."

"Occam's Razor?" Ahab asked.

Anna nodded.

"The simplest answer is probably the correct one," she said. "We brainstormed hundreds of scenarios. We figured it must be a glitch on the other end. We couldn't initiate a transfer back to O221 from this side so we were dependent on the main facility."

"Right," Nick continued. "So, we tried to conserve our supplies. Conserve food. Conserve ammo. Conserve clothing. We thought we might have to live our lives out here."

Alex "Beef" Scott nodded.

"Plus, you probably shouldn't go hunting those maniacs in the first place," he said.

Damon had been fiddling with the distress beacon.

"Commanders," Damon said. "Let's all crowd around over here."

They had discussed this with Angus before leaving. They would shut the beacon off and then reactivate it, taking advantage of the image imbedded in the signal. Angus wasn't sure if it would work – and work consistently – but it was worth a shot. Damon wrote a quick note on a piece of paper with a thick permanent marker. All seven people crowded into what they hoped would be a "picture" – Cadey, Damon, Alex, Rick, Anna, Nick and Davis.

"Okay, here we go," Cadey reached over and activated the "broadcast" feature of the unit.

They were instructed to wait five minutes before shutting the unit off again.

"Anything else we should know?" Beef asked.

"Aside from the fish monster?" Anna said, smiling. "No. Not really."

* *

Time passed in Objekt 221 with the same regularity that it did in Ancient Crimea.

"One second here equals one second there," Angus said as he and AJ walked into the small computer room, COMM4, he had originally heard the distress beacon.

"I read a book once where every time someone goes through a time rift, they appear at the same time, say September 1st, 1970. That's where the time jump starts. No matter how long he stays there, he comes back to the present, he goes back five years later in the present and he's back on September 1st, 1970," AJ said.

"Sure," Angus replied, putting his bag of chips down on one computer workstation. "That works for that particular narrative. In our reality, though, O221 and Gamma Complex are always separated by exactly 100 million years. To the second. Even though a day or year might take roughly a different amount of time. Due to the wobble in the Earth's circuit around the sun, for example. 100 million years. One second here equals one second there."

"So, they've been over there for," AJ checked her watch, "for two hours and 25 minutes."

"Yup."

They had been searching through various computer files in this room since the excursion team left. They were doing their checklist-mandated due diligence, but also looking for any information on why a team of researchers might have been left in the distant past.

They had found passing references to Facility 3, Facility 4, Building 5 and The Ruins. They were data-mining various systems to locate any additional info.

"I remember we were building a prototype smart house about seven years ago," Angus said as they were settling in. "Project J.E.N.I. Total A.I. immersion. Everything was wired. Toaster. Closet doors. Your mailbox would analyze that day's post and tell you … *Angus, you have your Bank USA statement and a birthday card from your mortgage company.* It was pretty cool."

"Cool," AJ said. "But I'm wondering at the relevance."

"It's one of those corporate things. We pulled funding. I was just thinking about what if some new company came in and tried to sift through our files to figure out who Jenny was. We had started to adopt a sort of corporate shorthand when discussing that project. I can only imagine the simple stuff we're overlooking on this Ancient Crimea stuff because of idiot acronyms or pet names they'd have given things."

"It's like amnesia," AJ said.

"What are you …?" Angus started and stopped because the workstation that had been set up to monitor the Cretaceous distress signal began chirping.

* *

Davis was pressing keys on the main console monitor and a map of the area surrounding Hell Island popped up. He zoomed out a bit and re-centered the image where he wanted it. The image took up a large section of the window HUD. They were in the command center

– basically the floor above the huge conference room with the giant curved windows. The center section of the window was the map.

Davis walked up to the window; he held a computer tablet in his left hand.

"This is us and this is Gamma Complex," he said, pointing to first one and then a second feature on the map. "Five miles apart. We were lucky earlier, but now, later in the day, we're getting on feeding time. There's about three more hours of daylight before most of the nastiness goes to sleep. But not all. So it gives us two options."

He had drawn a straight line from Facility Four to the rift entry point in Gamma. The line said FIVE MILES across it.

"We'll be passing through these feeding zones." Davis pressed a few keys on his computer tablet and several sections popped up on the map. They were highlighted in various colors and various notations. Also, several diamond icons emerged with "Last Known Location" headings. "Feeding zones plus last known locations of the Goliath family members."

"That's not promising," Cadey said.

"There's a shortcut across the water," Davis pressed a few more keys and a new line appeared, connecting Hell Island to Gamma Complex by first going across a small section of the Black Sea and then finishing the trek across land. The line had THREE MILES stenciled across it. "As you can see. The curve of the shore. We'd cut all that out."

Alex noted a section of land a couple of miles on the other side of Gamma labeled "The Ruins", but didn't say anything.

"The JLTVs in their current configuration are not amphibious at that depth and they certainly don't float," Davis continued. "So, we'd have to take the boats. And deal with Nessie."

"Nessie?" Cadey asked.

"The fish monster," Anna said.

"Great," Damon said.

"Anything we can do with the Ruins?" Alex asked.

There was silence in the room for a moment.

"Well that's," Anna said, "that's an interesting story."

CHAPTER 8

NOCTURNAL SCAVENGER. GAMMA-CLASS.

ANGUS HAD BEEN interrupted mid-thought as the beacon monitor in the sub-control room COMM4 started beeping. He hopped up and walked directly to that computer to activate the sleeping program.

It was the exact same application that had caught his attention two days ago. He ran a cable from the computer to his own laptop.

"Is that them?" AJ asked.

"Looks like it," Angus said. "At the very least, they've reset the broadcast. Let's see if a new image was sent."

Since he had solved the problem once before, it was easy to decode the seemingly incomprehensible data stream a second time. He could then find out if there was a start-up image embedded in this signal as well.

"Boom," Angus said, doing finger-guns at the monitor. He would have done it if alone, and was a bit ashamed to remember that AJ was in the room with him. He turned the laptop so she could see the screen head-on. It was a grainy image of the seven team members. Damon held up a small sign. **Found team. Coming back**. And the local date and time.

"Five minutes ago," Angus said, comparing his watch to the Ancient Crimea clock that was running in the upper right-hand corner of his laptop screen.

"Great," AJ said. "Everything's going according to plan."

"That's," Angus said, smiling, "when disaster usually strikes."

"I suppose so," AJ said. "Hey. Did you see any references to the Ruins? I found what looks like a map, but there's no legend. And no description."

"Hmm," he said. "Let's have a look."

As Angus wheeled his bulk over to a new workstation, AJ took out her cell phone, sent a quick text message, deleted the string, and put it back in her pocket.

* *

"The Ruins can't help you," Davis said as they were putting the finishing touches on packing up the triplet of JLTVs to bring everything back to Gamma Complex. "But I can tell you what happened there. It was four months ago. Give or take."

* *

It was an eight-person excursion – five researchers and three members of the Allied Genetics private security force. The team was run by "The Sarge." No one was sure if that was his operational callsign or his rank in the military. Everyone simply called him The Sarge. He was average height and thick across the chest and arms. He was in his early 50s and rumor had it that he had served in the Marines. He led two younger soldiers – Onion and Spiral – and the five scientists out of Gamma Complex and into the morning sun.

The two younger security men had left first and secured the two Light Strike Vehicles (LSVs) from the huge garage. They were essentially dune-buggies with a few strategically-placed pieces of armor plating. The small vehicles were painted a matte orange that blended in with absolutely nothing.

The eight team members piled into the two vehicles and they sped off to the East.

"Here you go," Charles Cove, the leader of the researchers spoke. He was manipulating his wrist computer and swiping along the image. Each swipe sent some data to a corresponding receiver. "I've made some slight alterations to the plan. This pattern should be slightly more efficient. In and out."

They were on a mapping excursion. Purely passive – no extraction. They were part three of a three-part plan and would be mapping the final corridor of a series of buildings known as "The Ruins".

Leaving Gamma Complex in the distance, the excursion was actually driving along a section of land called "the road."

The road had been their first indication that the Cretaceous held clues not only about undiscovered dinosaurs, but evidence about a super-ancient civilization. Allied Genetics had been sending researchers back in an effort to document what had clearly been a section of a constructed highway, a large building – referred to as Building 5 because one character in what was left of a string of characters on the outside of the building looked similar to the number five – and a group of six smaller buildings that sat across the road from both Gamma Complex and B5.

Allied had planned on starting an excavation project early next year with the hopes of gaining a better understanding of this civilization that would be completely erased by the time Humanity 2.0 came to power 100 million years in the future.

The truth was, it was more important for the company to gather as much information as they could while the rift was still proprietary. As soon as they announced their findings, they would be overrun by the world's scientific community – their status as a private corporation notwithstanding. They would be forced to open their door to Ancient Crimea to the planet at large. Their cadre of lawyers had already run many mock-courts to see how the legislation would likely proceed. Allied was having enough trouble protecting their dozens of non-disclosure agreements … their understanding of the Cretaceous and Ancient Earth was a ticking intellectual timebomb.

"Okay," Sarge said. "Heads outta asses. Eyes up."

They had arrived at the Ruins.

* *

"Have you been over in Building 5? Seen that statue?" Davis Brighton and Charles Cove were teamed up for this survey. They were trailed by one of the soldiers known only as "Onion." Sarge had taken up position by the two vehicles as a mini-overwatch. Researchers Anna Tobin, Art Beech and Nick Jennings were joined by the final security man – Spiral – as they searched the other section of buildings.

Cove was set to explore buildings A, B and C while Anna would search D, E and F. The pattern Cove had devised had them all proceed around each other, never meeting until coming together back at the two cars.

"The Picasso Woman?" Cove answered back and shook his head. "Not really. I saw some documentation, but I haven't been over there to look in person, yet. The proportions are all weird, right?"

The two men had entered Building B, the first on their list. The six buildings in the small community were all different sizes and had reached various levels of deterioration. None of them, even in their prime, seemed to be as big as the imposing Building 5 which was clearly visible across the huge swath of flat land, the road, which separated these two sections of super-ancient civilization.

In the quiet, they could hear the waves lapping at the shore. The land just past the Ruins fell away in a 30-foot cliff into the surging waters of the Black Sea.

"The proportions are strange in the statue, yes," Davis said. "But I think they are accurate to the period. I caught a glimpse of the bio-report. They're saying Humanity 1.0 might have averaged over seven feet tall. Based on not only the statue, but the door-frames and the stone steps in the auditorium."

They continued through Building B; the laser-survey equipment was taking hyper-accurate readings of the area. Both men were manipulating their own equipment via hand-held computer tablets.

"I'm showing this doorway as four-feet wide," Cove said. "A foot wider than the standard ADA width."

"See? Wonder why they were so much bigger?"

"What was *that*?" came the voice of Onion, the security officer who stood off to their right. He was loud and clear over their faceplate speakers.

A small figure had darted across their field of vision as they stood in one room facing the back room, the final room to be surveyed, in Building B. All three of their faceplate HUDs had lit up immediately as the digital sensors processed the half-lit image quicker than the three men's eyes and brains could have.

NR-401G.

It was an average-sized nocturnal predator. The dino was three-feet tall with a too-short tail. The tail was a source of great debate among Allied scientists. Was it a weapon? A failure of evolutionary science? It was only a foot long and sharpened to a deadly point. No one had yet observed the 401G using its tail as a weapon. As the sun streamed in through the shattered ceiling of Building B, they could see the brilliant brown skin of the reptile, highlighted by the thick brown and yellow bristles of the mohawk hair that ran from the crown of his head to the middle of his back.

The faceplate sensors could no longer track the small beast – they were hindered by the thick, ancient version of concrete the super-ancient civilization had used. The sensors were calibrated against modern materials. Onion had unholstered a pistol and stepped around the two scientists. He was about to enter the final room and see if he could locate the small dinosaur.

Onion stepped into the room and as soon as his right foot hit the floor, they were all shocked by the shout that came over the faceplate speaker system.

"Hive," the voice called. "Building D."

The team comm channel had exploded in a burst of activity as the three soldiers ran toward Building D and were calling out locations. Building D was the final building nearest the cliff overlooking the water.

Spiral was there first, as his team had called out the warning. Onion and Sarge appeared seconds later. Sarge had driven one of the LSVs around the perimeter of the area and parked it between Building D and the cliff's edge. He pulled a heavy weapon out of the rear storage and called into his faceplate microphone.

"What do we have?"

He saw his two security men highlighted on the HUD map and walked to them.

"Back of the building, sir," Spiral said. "Looks like the entire back half of D is a nest. NR-401G."

"Okay," Sarge said.

"We also saw one just before the warning went out. Building B, sir," Onion also reported.

"Okay," Sarge said. "Looks like they've turned this into their own habitat." He paused, reading the 401G's stats off his HUD. He read the finer points out loud. "Nocturnal scavenger. Gamma-class. Hasn't exhibited pack hunting characteristics. Categorized." And then he read the date and the lead researcher's name. The 401G had been first observed six months prior. "Suggestions?"

He turned to Charles Cove, who was leading the mission from the perspective of the science ranks. The brains to Sarge's brawn.

"This is a change to the mission parameters," he said. "We could go remote survey, drones, or, possibly, come back at night when they would likely evacuate the habitat. In any event, we should probably reset."

"Jesus," Sarge said.

"We were able to survey E and F," Anna offered.

Davis nodded.

"We got most of B."

"So, we got nearly half through," Sarge said. He thought for a moment. "Okay. We take what we've got for now, upload it. Put together a different plan. Right?"

"Agreed," Charles said. "There's no way to work around them right now?"

Cove was looking at his wrist monitor, watching the video from Nick's HUD, the first person to see the hive.

"This looks pretty extensive," he said. "And we saw one on the other side of the complex. There's no telling how many there are. They haven't exhibited pack aggression, but like any nocturnal predator, they'll be fiercely protective of their home – especially while trying to get some sleep."

"The one we saw could have been a scout," Davis offered. "On his way to wake everyone up right now."

Sarge nodded.

"My first instinct is to wipe them out, but that's not the way we're supposed to proceed." He paused. "Let's get back to base."

He turned away from the building and was immediately knocked to his feet by two NR-401Gs. They came rocketing out from behind Building D and must have identified him as the leader of the group. Possibly an instinct. Possibly by the way he was standing. Possibly the four-foot long weapon he was holding. For whatever reason, they leapt at him and struck him with such force that he was knocked backward six feet and fell to the ground.

Just as Sarge was getting his bearings and crawling back to his feet, another 15 dinos burst from the shadows both inside Building D and from around various corners. The researchers scattered, and the two security men stood back to back and opened fire. They were able to drop one of the 401Gs before they were overrun. One of the reptiles did something not yet caught on video – running full speed ahead, the 401G turned sideways in a hop and used his blunt tail to whip past Onion. The point of his tail caught the soldier right in the groin and cut him right down to the bone.

Onion howled in pain, and everyone's faceplate HUD carried the warning. Not only was Onion's suit punctured, but his groin had become a waterfall of blood. He went into shock and died from the combination of blood loss and oxygen deprivation.

Charles Cove, unfortunately, was the slowest of the researchers and was soon attacked by a pack of the reptiles. Three of them pounced on the frightened man as he unholstered his own sidearm. While their teeth couldn't pierce the reinforced acrylic of his faceplate, the three combined to work on his abdomen.

For his part, Sarge had finally struggled back to his feet and was trying desperately to catch his breath. The rest of the team could hear him wheezing over their speakers. He couldn't find the huge assault rifle, and just as he stood wavering, the same two 401Gs that had initially struck him had lined up for a second shot. They both ran at him full speed and lowered their shoulders like battering rams. The force of the impact lifted him from the ground and the momentum carried him off the cliff into the waters of the Black Sea.

"Into the car," Spiral, now the lone remaining security officer, called over the faceplate microphone. The four remaining researchers were nearest the LSV that Sarge had driven to the back of the complex, so they started running in that direction. Spiral, unfortunately, had meant the LSV on the other side of the Ruins. He started running in that direction and was immediately overrun by a group of 401Gs. In so doing, essentially, Spiral sacrificed himself as a distraction so the researchers had a clear shot at the bright orange vehicle.

As he was torn apart, he never said a word.

* *

"I think you can slow down now," Davis Brighton said.

Researcher Anna Tobin was the closest to the driver's side of the LSV, so she got behind the wheel and sped out of the small clearing behind the Ruins. She turned left when she reached the road and floored it out of the area. They had been chased for a short distance by what looked like 40 of the medium-sized nocturnal reptiles. They had sped past the Gamma Complex façade because it looked like the T-Rexes who fed in that general vicinity were already awake.

So, they kept driving and thought about what to do.

"When is O221 initiating the call-back?" Arlington Beech asked the car in general.

"Another 45 minutes," Anna answered. "We could initiate an emergency return."

"I think only Charles and the Sarge had the code," Davis said.

"How is *that* a good idea?" Nick Jennings asked.

"It's just protocol," Davis answered. "We can get back into the building and wait for the main facility to initiate our return."

Anna nodded.

"That's probably for the best." She had been slowing down slightly since Davis suggested it, but she had kept her head on a swivel. Even though she knew they wouldn't have chased her the three or four miles they had driven, she was concerned about a group of NR-401Gs exploding out of the foliage and overrunning their vehicle. She was still astonished at how quickly they had moved as a group.

"Hey, what's that?" Nick asked from the back seat, pointing to the front and left of the vehicle. "To the left. Above those trees."

It was a huge, circular building.

"Is that Hell Island?" Davis asked, more to himself than the other researchers.

* *

"Yep," Davis continued his story in the present setting.

They had finished loading the three huge JLTVs and were piling in as he completed the tale.

"So, you had never been here before that?" Damon asked.

Davis shook his head even though Damon wasn't in visual range of him.

"Allied, bizarrely, kept data compartmentalized," Cadey answered over the speakers. "There were groups who knew of the two pads, but didn't know about the vehicle garage. Groups who knew about Gamma and Facility 4, but had no idea about the Ruins."

"Right," Anna answered. "I figure there have to be at least two more facilities out here ... if Gamma is Facility 1 and Hell Island is Facility 4 ... it just makes sense."

"So, we went back to Gamma and waited for the home base to initialize the rift," Davis wound up his story. "But it never happened. From what I've gathered, that might have been around the time the whole facility was on lockdown."

"Yeah," Alex said. "Sorry about that."

"It was bound to happen," Nick said. "Play with fire, and all that. How 'bout we go home?"

"Sold," Cadey Park said, smiling.

CHAPTER 9

THE TRUNCATED CONVOY SPED OFF

TWENTY-ONE PEOPLE JAMMED into the three JLTVs and began the long trek back to Gamma Complex and, finally, Objekt 221. The small convoy rumbled out from under the Hell Island facility and continued down the path toward the big moat. The steel bridge dropped into place and then raised back up again once they were safely across. The lead truck, piloted by Alex "Beef" Scott, exited the peninsular pathway and turned right – back to the high-tech launching pad.

"Stay frosty," Alex called out over the faceplate microphone. "I've been informed that we're half-way through the final stage of the feeding period. All these guys are going to want to be heading home. Let's not give them an appetizing target."

"Copy that," answered both Damon Butcher, in the second vehicle, and Rick "Ahab" Everson in the trail position.

Each truck was carrying a combination of military and researchers as well as one each of the three missing scientists. They were also carrying the various crates of supplies the team had brought from O221 at the outset of the rescue operation and, in addition, a crate of the missing scientists' personal belongings which amounted to data storage since they were generally wearing everything they actually owned.

"Hey," Alex exclaimed and jerked the wheel of the truck to the right. Damon followed suit as did Ahab. Unfortunately, Ahab's defensive driving maneuver failed miserably. His JLTV was struck broadside by a huge beast running at full speed. The military vehicle was strong, but never stood a chance against the enormous bulk and the organic plating.

The truth is, the beast never saw them.

The windshield HUDs of all three vehicles lit up in synch. The dinosaur was a Wuerhosaurus – assumed to be the last relative of the Stegosaurus. It was 23 feet long and weighed four tons – almost 9,000 pounds. The dino was a dark green and walked on all fours. He had tree-trunks for legs and a thick, heavy neck. There were blunt armored body plates that ran from the back of his head all the way to his relatively short tail. He was as big as if not bigger than the giant military vehicle, but struck it full-force – similar to a car running a stop light and blasting directly into the side of another vehicle.

A classic T-bone collision. Ahab's truck shuddered and slid sideways after the impact.

"Hold on," he said, muscling the steering wheel as he tried to regain control. Unfortunately, he did not. As he steered away from the skid and away from the cliff-edge – only protected here by short shrubbery – the balance of the big vehicle tipped, then over-compensated and then they rolled over.

Once, twice.

And then, over the cliff.

* *

Alex, in the lead vehicle, couldn't tell what happened. His HUD was providing him all sorts of warning klaxons, but he wasn't seeing any sort of rear-view camera. By the time he had activated it, the action was over, and Ahab was gone.

* *

Despite their size, the JLTVs had some built-in buoyancy. They could never be used as a boat, but they would stay afloat long enough for their inhabitants to get clear. While their momentum had carried them almost 90 feet from the shore, the JLTV bobbed gently on the surface.

"Everyone out," Ahab called. "Leave the cargo. We're alive, Beef. Just a little wet."

"Copy that, Ahab," Alex said over the faceplate speakers. "We'll circle around to your exit point."

Anna Tobin was in the truck that was in the water.

"The excursion suits are water-tight," she said to Ahab in specific, but to the team in general. "But I wouldn't recommend we test our luck."

"Understood," Rick said. "Topside. Double-quick."

The heavy, armored doors were half submerged and it would take an enormous amount of pressure to push them open against the undulating water. The military, of course, had a contingency plan in place. The custom-built JLTV's electronics system was completely encased in waterproof tubing. The power wouldn't stay on indefinitely, but they had time to assess their situation and hit the powered lock release on the door windows. They didn't raise and lower like a passenger vehicle – but could be cranked outward to foster the occupants' escape.

Two at a time, one through each door window, the excursion team escaped into the frigid water.

And sunk to the sea bed. Like a stone.

The enviro outfits were built to be air-tight and waterproof, more to account for the violent rainstorms that an excursion team could face. They were never designed to be effective swimming suits.

"Okay," Ahab said to both his immediate team and the rest of the team on dry land. "So, I guess we walk."

"What the hell's that?" asked a voice from the other side of the floating JLTV. From their perspective, the vehicle was floating about four feet from the sandy floor of the Black Sea – its wheels lazily turning against the churning water. The voice was Dave "Blue" Green and he was pointing back toward Hell Island.

Ahab walked to Dave's side of the vehicle as the rest of the team exited the vehicle. Soon, everyone was on the passenger side of the JLTV. Enhanced by night vision, thermal imaging and penetrative sonar, the HUD was showing them what was underneath the Hell Island facility.

It was a long, thin row of plate windows. An observation deck. An underwater observation deck. It was shocking to see for numerous reasons, one of which was that the room behind the heavy acrylic windows was lit brightly. The extreme corners of the observation area were caked in barnacles and algae and other water-based grime.

"Is that a door?" Ahab asked himself.

To the right of their HUD was a door, perhaps to a maintenance airlock, that was completely free of rust, dirt or marine life. It looked like it had recently been opened.

Instinctively, Ahab took a step toward the hidden location. He was immediately stopped by the warning klaxons in his armor.

WARNING! CRETOXYRHINA DETECTED!

The text was flashing in red. The descriptive portion of the HUD filled in with notes and Rick Everson was able to pull out certain phrases. Shark ancestor. Hunting style similar to great white. Razor-sharp, three-inch long teeth. Thirty feet long. Burst speeds over 40 miles per hour.

The faceplate digitally outlined a giant shark pacing just past the observation window – just over a third of a mile away.

"Time to go," Anna said, as calmly and quickly as she could. "Steady rate. They have good eyesight. Let's not give him anything to stare at."

Unfortunately, its attention had already been caught by the huge truck that crashed through the underbrush and launched itself into the water not five minutes ago. The prehistoric shark was swimming, lateral to the excursion team, almost as if he was studying them out of his peripheral vision.

The seven people – a mixture of researchers and soldiers – began moving toward the cliff, the edge of the water. They didn't have any projectile weapons that would fire while submerged, so, those who were equipped, pulled out various hunting and combat knives. It was essentially a psychological trick.

"Whistling through the graveyard," Mark "Thunder" Wilson said as he noticed everyone doing it. He was a Wraith employee with three years of experience in the outfit. He had pulled his own black KA-BAR knife from a lumbar holster. Everyone, he noticed, was walking backward as they kept an active eye on the huge shark.

The team had to move a third the length of a football field to be safe – or at least whatever approximation of safe Ancient Crimea was willing to provide them.

"Sit rep?" Beef asked over the radio.

"We have a bogey in the water," Ahab answered, still moving backward. "Single target. Half a click away. Vehicle is submerged. Walking to land. Maybe five minutes."

"Copy that, Ahab," Beef answered. "We've established a perimeter. Over and out."

"Uh oh," Anna said, quietly, but with an underlying hint of panic.

The shark had turned toward them.

* *

Angus had always found it easier to complete paperwork with some sort of snack in front of him. Also, changing scenery somehow helped. As such, AJ found herself sitting across from Angus at a round, black table in the corner of the Level 3 cafeteria. Angus was going through various reports and made it a point to check his watch every five minutes.

"We're going to set the transpo to "accepting" as soon as we finish with this," he said.

"Why isn't it always accepting a transport?" AJ asked. "Especially given this situation with four "lost" researchers back in Ancient Crimea?"

Angus nodded.

"Yeah, that's a terrific question. And it really gets to the heart of the matter." He paused for a moment. "I'm not sure I've uncovered an actual policy, but I think it's set to some sort of manual control because they don't want a velociraptor stepping onto the launching pad and accidentally being sent 100 million years into his future. He might not live for long in our atmosphere, but he could certainly cause problems while alive."

AJ nodded in return.

"I guess that makes sense."

Angus went back to his paperwork. AJ pulled out her cell phone and started a text conversation. Or continued one. It was impossible for Angus to tell, but he didn't bring it up.

Several moments passed in silence and Angus checked his watch again. Wordlessly, he collected his paperwork and stood up to leave. AJ also stood. She dumped her trash in the bin near them and made an involuntary Huh noise.

"What is it?" Angus also tossed his garbage.

"Someone tossed a bag of chipotle-cheddar flavored potato chips," she said. "It's like the third different product I've seen with that flavoring this week. Halo effect."

They turned to leave. When they got out into the hallway, they turned right and started walking to the control room elevator.

"Halo effect?" Angus asked.

"Yeah," she said. "Like you don't notice something and then you do. And then it's all over the place. You're only now noticing its commonality."

Angus shook his head.

"I think you mean the Baader-Meinhof Phenomenon," he said. "The Halo Effect is certainly a perceptive phenomenon but it deals more with personality traits. For example, you notice someone letting a cashier *keep the change*, and you ascribe positive characteristics to that person that might not otherwise exist. *He's a good person*, you tell yourself, because you witnessed a single good event. That single good event has created a personality halo around an individual who might habitually punch babies."

"Really?"

"Quite," Angus said. "You're more referring to Baader-Meinhof or the illusion of frequency effect. It's more commonly known as the Blue Car Syndrome. You buy a blue car and suddenly you see scads of blue cars on the road. Certainly, more than you ever noticed before."

"How 'bout that?"

"It's an interesting phenomenon," Angus said, "but, then again, diseases of perception usually are."

They had arrived at the rift's control room and took chairs at workstations in the same row, but on opposite sides of the main aisle.

"Alright," Angus said, cracking his knuckles in dramatic fashion. "Let's get our team home."

If he noticed AJ rolling her eyes, he didn't mention it.

* *

Vehicles one and two had both backed into position right near the spot that vehicle three had left dry land. Damon figured out how to split-screen the windshield HUD into front-facing and rear-facing, and had shared the information with Alex Scott, who was piloting the other vehicle. All of the passengers were dead silent.

The faceplate HUDs had a small screen, a feed of what Ahab was seeing under the Black Sea. They had all seen the red outline of the prehistoric shark turn and start swimming toward the underwater excursion.

"This can't be happening," Cadey Park said.

* *

2,000 feet.

Their faceplate HUDs were blinking ominously. The cretoxyrhina had turned toward them and was starting to close the distance from the underwater Hell Island view screen to the crashed JLTV.

WARNING. WARNING.

"Okay," Ahab said. "We need to pick up the pace."

The seven submerged team members had been slowly walking backward through the waters of the ancient Black Sea. They had moved some distance but were still more than 60 feet from the water's end. They knew that the shark had a burst speed of more than 40 miles an hour but they had been trying to appear as uninteresting as possible. Unfortunately, the plan had not worked.

"Double-time it," Anna said, echoing Ahab's sentiment.

Half the team turned and started moving as quickly as possible. They were still water-tight and had plenty of breathing air. They were only in 10 feet of water, so there were no pressurization issues. Unfortunately, they were trying to run underwater wearing several pounds of tactical environmental suit engineering.

1,500 feet.

Five of the team had turned and attempted to speed up by moving forward and two members continued moving backward, always keeping eyes on the swiftly approaching shark. The predator seemed to pause in mid-air and shot forward with a powerful, aggressive sweep of his tail. He seemed to hunch his back and somehow create a downhill gravity.

The faceplate HUD gave a quick error message and then read out 200 feet.

The burst attack was over, but the shark was still moving quickly toward the team. His glowing outline was getting larger and larger on Ahab's HUD. Only he and Anna continued walking backward. Suddenly, the shark veered to his left – the team's right and swept past Ahab. The wake of the movement was enough to cause him to lose balance and fall to the sandy, muddy ground. Anna turned to watch the shark rip past them and go straight for the two people on the far side of the formation.

Anna could see it in slow motion. The shark rotated slightly to his left and his eyes rolled back for protection – just like a modern-day great white. With another mighty sweep of his tail, the cretoxyrhina jerked forward and grabbed two members of the excursion team, turned further left and disappeared along the coast.

The two men screamed into their faceplate mics. The team channel automatically quieted the sound, but the HUD showed an alert for the researcher Sven Stegner and Wraith Donny "Rufus" Arnoldson. Their bio-readings spiked and then fell flat. During the attack, Anna had frozen in place. None of the rest of the team had actually seen what happened. They all saw the warning and stopped. The two men who were right next to them were suddenly gone.

WARNING! TEAM MEMBER "STEGNER!" FLATLINE.

WARNING! TEAM MEMBER "RUFUS!" FLATLINE.

Ahab clambered to his feet and grabbed Anna's arm.

"We have to move," he said and turned away from her.

Everyone, then, had started running underwater. It would have been comical had it not been so frightening.

With the shark feeding some distance off, they made it to the shallow water and, eventually the 10 feet of sand that rose dramatically to the cliff's edge.

"Now, we climb," Ahab said, taking a deep breath.

* *

The cliff ascension took nearly as long as the underwater march had but, fortunately, it passed without incident. Beef, Damon and the rest of the remaining excursion team watched their slow progress through 14 sets of HUD monitors.

Those who sat in the front seats of the two stationary JLTVs kept alternating their watchful gazes from the team members climbing up the cliff face to the slowly setting sun and the new horrors the darkness might bring. They had barely made it off the Hell Island entrance bridge before being violently side-tracked. They still had several miles of terrain separating them from Gamma Complex. Now they were down one vehicle, two team members and an unknown amount of weaponry in the lost storage crates.

For their part, the ascension team was taking it slow. Between the jutting rocks and tree roots, the two-story climb wasn't too intimidating. Unfortunately, some of the handholds ended up being jagged rocks that threatened to puncture various parts of the environmental suits. The suits had proven durable, but they had just been dunked in the Black Sea for a significant amount of time. It was impossible to tell if any seams or junctions were weakened. There was an unspoken understanding to not put any more undue stress on the gear.

Cresting the cliff, Rick "Ahab" Everson took several deep breaths to gather himself – standing, bent forward with the palms of his heavy gloves resting on his thighs. His eyes flicked to the small portion of the HUD that tracked his personal vital signs. Pulse and respiration rate were way above his baseline measurements. A small warning light was blinking next to these vitals.

"Can it, Poindexter," he said under his breath. Ahab rolled his shoulders to crack his back and snapped his head from side to side to crack his neck. He turned to watch the other four members of his JLTV crew heave themselves up over the edge of the cliff.

"Let's go, sissy," Beef called over the faceplate speakers. "You can tell me all about the scary fish who was mean to you over a beer at O221. I'm buying."

Ahab laughed as he reached forward and helped researcher Anna Tobin to her feet.

"Copy that," he answered.

* *

The truncated convoy sped off. There were seven members of the team in the lead car, Car A, driven by Damon Butcher. There were seven members of the team in the second car, Car B, driven by Alex Scott. The remaining five team members including Ahab Everson and Anna Tobin were arranged around the outside of Car B. There were two people along the driver's side and three along the passenger's side. They stood on the diamond-plate running boards and clung to the roof-rack as the excursion team made a valiant effort, in the setting sun, to get back to Gamma Complex and, thus, back to present day.

"A great white shark?" Ahab asked as the two trucks sped along the prairie. It was Anna Tobin who answered, also clinging to the side of Car B. She was more familiar with manipulating the faceplate and wrist-mounted computers. She pulled up the warning screen and shared the information across the team.

"Sort of," she said. "Cretoxyrhina. A mackerel shark. Fossils have been found all over the world. This one seemed a little longer than the assumed average of 26 feet."

"It's pretty common," Davis responded from inside Car A. "We're finding that most of our assumptions were slightly off. Generally, what we're seeing in the field is bigger than we expected."

"Terrific," Ahab said. "This one looked like a great white."

Anna nodded, if only to herself.

"That's true. They're quite similar in appearance and hunting patterns. Cretoxyrhina had a much faster burst speed, though."

"No joke."

"Generally, they eat large fish, mosasaurs, plesiosaurs and, well, anything unlucky enough to fall into their water," Nick Jennings said from inside Car B. He shrugged to himself. "Sorry."

"So, stay out of the water," Ahab said. "Got it."

While driving, Beef was manipulating the control surface of his wrist computer. After a moment, he found what he was looking for and highlighted a command function. His HUD lit up – Private Channel Established. Local Only.

"Ahab."

"Ready," came the response from Ahab directly to Beef's speakers.

"We're going to need to debrief about that underwater facility."

"Copy that," Ahab said. "It sure looked, um, *in use*."

Alex "Beef" Scott nodded to himself while behind the wheel of the huge JLTV.

"And I think we both know who is using it," he said, and then reached up to press another button on his wrist-mounted computer. "We'll talk to French when we get back. Disabling private channel."

"Copy," Ahab said.

He looked around at the surroundings and then to each of his team members. He last looked at Anna Tobin, one of the Allied Genetics researchers who had been trapped in Ancient Crimea for four months after a dino attack. How much about Allied's true movements was she privy to? How much had they actually explored Hell Island?

Damon had been given orders from Angus to download operational files, but had they been sanitized? What if the four missing researchers had orders of their own? They had months to themselves with a generous store of food, water and other provisions.

Four months.

And they just now activated a distress beacon?

What had they been doing in that time?

Ahab was pulled out of his silent conspiracy-theory-driven reverie by a harsh buzzing sound inside his helmet. A warning klaxon. His HUD flashed in bright orange.

WARNING! UC-0104 "GOLIATHS" DETECTED!

"Oh, come on," he said to himself and the entire rest of the excursion team. He turned his head to look behind the small convoy. "Wonderful."

Three of the dangerous hybrid Goliaths were bounding along behind the JLTVs. They were scary enough on their own but the research video the excursion team had watched mere minutes ago put the monster in an entirely different context.

* *

Alex Scott was watching the action unfold on his rear-facing monitor that took up a small, translucent section of his windshield. The three six-legged super-predators were running after the military convoy. They were keeping pace but not gaining on the two vehicles. Beef noted, absently, that the running Goliaths were more similar to the musculature and movement of a gorilla than that of a horse. They were about 20 yards behind the chase vehicle and were galloping along in formation using their hind legs and all four arms in a smooth motion.

"Weapons free," Ahab said.

In this situation, being carried along on the outer shell of the JLTV was both a blessing and a curse. They were exposed to not only the elements, but to attack. However, as this version of the military transport had no external weapons, they could be an aggressive defensive force to counter an onslaught. For his part, Ahab pulled the Sledgehammer shotgun off the magnetic clip on his back and prepared to fire. He had moved to the rear-most position on the driver's side. He had nodded to the Wraith soldier, Mark "Thunder" Wilson, who moved to the same position on the opposite side of the vehicle.

Thunder took an MP-5 submachine gun from a thigh holster. It wasn't the biggest caliber weapon he was carrying, but it was the most damage he could do firing with only one hand. Ahab wouldn't have that problem with the AA-12 as it was specifically designed to absorb recoil.

The two men began firing – Ahab at the Goliath on the right and Thunder at the Goliath on the left. With the first explosion from the Sledgehammer, the three dinos scattered. Apparently, there had been some level of societal communication. A warning about what had happened to the T-Rex earlier in the day. Perhaps, somehow, they could even recognize the weapon itself.

Or, possibly, Ahab was giving them too much credit. Maybe it wasn't intelligence or anthropomorphism … maybe they were just shocked by the sound. The Sledgehammer sounded like a war all by itself.

Ahab had stopped shooting when the dinos scattered. Thunder had fired his clip empty. He ejected the spent magazine and tried to grab a fresh clip. Unfortunately, he had lost a great deal of dexterity in the heavy, Kevlar environmental suits. In trying to switch hands, he lost his grip and dropped the SMG. It clattered along the ground behind the JLTV. He paused a moment in trying to decide if he should put the fresh mag back in the combat webbing along the front of his suit or just drop it along with the gun.

The pause cost him his life.

The left-most Goliath bounded back into position and accelerated faster than they thought was possible.

Watching his rear-view monitor, Alex "Beef" Scott's mouth was agape.

"Oh my God," he said.

The Goliath leapt directly at Thunder Wilson and bit him clean in half. Wilson's legs kicked spasmodically as his body – both halves of it – fell away from the JLTV. The Goliath landed gracefully and began to run back to his original position in the formation. Ahab, though, was ready.

WARNING! TEAM MEMBER "THUNDER!" FLATLINE.

"Not so fast, my friend," he said, and unloaded on the beast with the 32-shell drum of the Sledgehammer shotgun. Ten projectiles in, and the Goliath had been blown apart. Everyone watched it from Ahab's feed – the animal's corpse thumping away into the distance.

"Five down," came Anna's voice, quiet, on the team comm over the faceplate speakers.

The two remaining Goliaths fell back another 10 yards but continued to keep pace with the small military convoy. Damon sped up a few miles an hour. Even with a big, heavy military vehicle, they didn't want to risk axle damage speeding over rough, unknown terrain. Alex sped up also, staying five yards behind Car A.

The other Wraith soldier, Dave "Blue" Green, took up position on the back of the truck, opposite Ahab. Blue was holding a modified M-16 with under-barrel grenade launcher. He had looped a Velcro strap around the roof handhold for stability and was ready to fire his weapon unabated.

He nodded to his commander across the top of the vehicle. Ahab returned the nod.

* *

They were just inside a mile away from reaching Gamma Complex when Damon Butcher had a sudden, terrifying insight.

"Why aren't they attacking?"

In the passenger seat, Davis Brighton shrugged.

"We sped up," he said. "Maybe we're going too fast."

Damon shook his head.

"No, they could reach us," he said. There was a pause. The two trucks rumbled forward. "They have a pretty obvious burst of speed."

"They're driving us," Beef said from Car B. "They're pushing us forward. Toward a fortified position."

At that moment, they knew they had lost. It was a basic military strategy. If you could direct a fleeing enemy into the teeth of your larger force, then you could squeeze them from both front and back.

As if on cue, Damon's windshield HUD lit up in the "danger orange" color.

WARNING! UC-0104 "GOLIATHS" DETECTED!

* *

From the passenger seat of Car A, Davis Brighton pulled up the map of the immediate area and had the computer highlight the various warnings. It was a highly detailed drawing with some blue features and orange notes about danger.

The large building for Gamma Complex was just under a mile straight ahead of them on their left. It was partially obscured by a large U-shaped copse of trees. There was a large, clear alley inside the U that looked almost like a parking lot on the cartoonish map. There were two large X's in the open end of the U that represented two Goliaths. Two more X's stood in a line perpendicular to the others directly in the path of the military convoy.

"Jesus," Damon said, sitting next to Davis in the front of Car A. "Do we plow through them?"

"Negative," Alex said from the driver's seat of Car B. "They're far too agile and we might put ourselves at risk."

"Correct," Ahab said from the rear of the chase vehicle. "We might need to get into a position they didn't anticipate."

Alex nodded his head. He reached forward and drew a curve, like a huge letter C that went down below the fortified position, curved back across the road and came up from behind the four waiting Goliaths. The changes to the HUD appeared on everyone's faceplate screen.

"We could break to the right, loop all the way down toward the cliff's edge and come back up and around to the back. It might give us an offensive chance as they re-orient," Alex sat back in his seat.

Davis shrugged.

"With absolutely no prep time and six of the most vicious dinosaurs your military dollars could create – I think it's about the best we can come up with."

"Gear up, everyone," Beef said over the main team comm. "The heaviest caliber you can carry. We're goin' in hot and it's gonna be a mess."

"Hoo-rah," Ahab said.

* *

Still moving in a tight convoy, the two JLTVs slightly shifted to a direct collision course with the right-most Goliath. Even the most stoic, veteran Wraith soldier was nervous about the upcoming interaction. They had too many people to exit the vehicle and enter the complex without a fight. They had seen what the Goliath had done to the T-Rex in live-time, had seen what the Goliath had done to Thunder Wilson on their faceplate monitors, and had heard about the predatory clinical trials that the commanders had watched at Hell Island.

Even with some of the deadliest combat weaponry the world had ever seen, they weren't confident.

They were close, now.

"We're in the conflict zone," Damon called over the faceplate comms. "One hundred yards."

"Copy that," answered Ahab and Beef at nearly the same time. Beef was still watching behind them – keeping an eye on the two chase Goliaths. They were maintaining distance, but they would likely advance the closer they got to their fortified position.

"Fifty yards," Damon called out.

"Prepare to cut right," Alex answered.

There was a slight pause as the huge vehicles churned dirt. Many of the combined excursion team made the sign of the cross. The rest checked to make sure their weapons were loaded, off any sort of safety mechanism, and ready to fire on full-auto.

"On my mark," Damon said. "Three. Two. One. Cut."

They had approached the two growling Goliaths with deadly force. All four had been standing at the ready. They almost seemed to be shifting their weight from leg to leg like a professional tennis player awaiting a serve ... or a boxer sizing up his opponent. They had driven past the two who were blocking the Gamma Complex entrance – intentional or not – and plowed straight toward the right-most Goliath – the one standing at the very bottom of the defensive L-shape.

On Damon's mark, the two JLTVs turned hard to the right – north – toward the cliff-edge. The Goliath was shocked but quickly recovered. He dove both laterally and forward – an angle toward the driver's side of Car A. There might have been a cultural awareness – a shared consciousness – about the vulnerability of various modern vehicles. He swiped all four sets of arm claws across the driver's side tires of the JLTV.

These were solid rubber tires with no air inside. As the Goliath raked his razor-sharp claws against the tires, however, he significantly damaged the rubber and chunks of material began flying off the vehicle.

The Goliath rolled out of the way and the two chase dinos fell back as they were calculating the new strategy. The two trucks had turned right, toward the water and had started making a wide, sweeping arc through the big prairie that separated Gamma Complex from both Building 5 and the Ruins. Car A was throwing chunks of rubber off both driver's side tires through the entire curve.

"Damage report?" Damon asked. From the follow position, Alex could see the tires.

"You're shedding rubber, Damon," Alex said. "Starting to list."

"Copy."

It was becoming more difficult to steer through the corner, but Damon was able to hold his line. He wasn't looking out that side of the vehicle, but from the passenger seat, Davis could see the Ruins, then the remnants of the road, then Building 5. At the top of the curve, Damon swerved right.

"Ditch," he called to Alex.

On the far side of the road, it must have been Humanity 1.0's version of a collapsed culvert. It was three feet wide and almost four feet deep. Damon was able to avoid it, but Car B wasn't so lucky. Alex hit the concrete ditch head on – his front passenger-side tire jarring violently against the sharp edge. The sudden, trembling motion caused the truck to jump and one of the scientists lost her grip on the top rail of Car B. She fell to the ground and was immediately set upon by one of the chase Goliaths.

She died terrified and screaming.

Inside the truck, the entire vehicle was shuddering. The steering wheel was almost jerked out of Alex's hands.

"We blew a tie rod," he called into the faceplate mic.

The JLTV was designed to minimize the impact of losing a front tire – but not in the middle of a huge curve across jungle terrain. He was still following the path but it was taking all his strength to hold the steering wheel in place. Eventually, the tie rod broke entirely and the tire turned completely sideways – perpendicular to the other three tires. It was digging a huge gouge into the dirt and slowing the progress of Alex's truck.

"They're gaining on us," Ahab called, still watching the chase dinos. The one had made quick work of the fallen researcher and had rejoined his partner in following the military convoy.

Both trucks were starting to slow down. The two tires on the driver's side of Car A were shredded and the vehicle was now driving on its rims. The passenger front tire of Car B was completely turned against the momentum of the JLTV.

"Mission is FUBAR," Alex said, continuing to wrestle control of the big vehicle. "We're going to have to take 'em on right here."

"I'll pull left," Damon said in response. "You go right."

"Copy that."

"Alright," Ahab called, feeling the adrenaline rush through his body. "Go heavy. Let's put these boys down."

The two JLTVs slid to a collective halt about 40 yards from the door of Gamma Complex – on the other side of a clump of trees. They were surrounded by six huge apex predators – genetically crafted dinosaurs the computer had dubbed Goliath. Everyone clambered out of the trucks. Two front doors. Two rear passenger doors. And a back gate. There was a momentary pause as everyone took a group breath.

One Goliath roared and jumped forward.

It was a bloodbath.

* *

For numerous strategic reasons, the first Goliath had identified Rick "Ahab" Everson as his primary target. It could have been because he recognized Rick as having gunned down the third chase dino. It could have been simple positioning as Rick stood at the far right of the formation. In any event, as the Goliath launched himself into the air, all six sets of claws pointed directly at Ahab; the Wraith soldier opened fire and emptied the remaining rounds of his 32-shell shotgun mag into the dino.

The flying dinosaur was ripped to shreds and fell to the ground a lifeless bloody mess.

Then all hell broke loose.

"Reloading," Ahab shouted and stepped back behind two other Wraiths to eject his spent drum and slot in a fresh one.

The sounds of gunfire filled the faceplate speakers. The air hung thick with smoke and the smell of burnt gunpowder. Only a small portion of the smell could penetrate the strong enviro filters, but those on the front lines were getting a hint of a complex odor. It was a fusion – a metallic sulfur with a burnt sugar undertone. The Wraith team immediately recognized the smell while the remaining researchers recoiled. For the members of the Wraith team who had served in combat, the smell was like home.

DuPree wasn't as lucky. The man they knew as "Chino" had elected to dual-wield the MP-5 submachine gun. Generally, he had elected to go for the option of putting as many bullets as possible onto the battlefield. When the Goliath had come rushing at him, he unloaded both clips at the dino. Many found their mark, but not nearly enough. The ferocity and momentum of the dinosaur carried it forward and, with a howl, he decapitated the soldier. The dino's undoing, however, came from pausing a moment to swipe across the chest of the fallen combatant. In that moment, "Hux" Hutchinson fired his Sledgehammer shotgun into the side of the Goliath's head. The shell tore off the back of the dino's head and the monster fell to the soft primeval ground with its legs twitching spasmodically.

The Wraiths had tightened their ranks. They were a dozen soldiers – 11 Wraiths joined by Damon Butcher – in a tight curl protecting the four remaining scientists which were Cadey Park and the three rescued researchers. The scientists were close to the two crippled JLTVs and the soldiers were facing away from the trucks. They faced the four surviving Goliaths that were ducking and dodging gunfire.

With a final spasm, the Goliath that Hux had nearly decapitated spun around kicking a pound of dirt up with its hind legs. Damon dove out of the way of the flailing tail and it caught a soldier who was guarding the left flank right across the side of his face. The young Wraith never saw it coming and he crumpled to the ground – his face a veil of blood behind the crushed acrylic faceplate.

From a crouch, Damon opened fire into the dying Goliath. After a dozen rounds from his Heckler & Koch G36 assault rifle, the beast finally lay still. He had fixed the weapon with a 100-round drum magazine from the storage crates. Not only was it more bullets, but he felt that the larger mag helped with its stability. Standing and firing on the next closest Goliath, Damon felt himself crossing the threshold of strategic fear into true anger. It was a dangerous line to cross on the battlefield – especially in the face of a superior or strategically formidable force – because, as a soldier, he had been trained to keep his cool. With a growl, he continued firing and started taking steps forward.

There were four remaining Goliaths, and Damon could see the corner of Gamma Complex just past them.

"We're advancing," Alex said. "Blue, grab those ammo bags."

"Mow 'em down," Ahab said. He had reloaded his Sledgehammer and was firing it in single-shot. He was trying to keep the surviving Goliaths in a tight group. The big dinos continued to dance and dodge. They seemed to be retreating in the face of the relentless machine-gun fire – but it was more than that.

"Careful," Damon said. There was something deceptive about their movements. It was clear that the Wraiths had become the superior force but he had seen the Goliath training in action. They were bred to be as brilliant as they were lethal. "I don't trust this."

The Wraiths were firing in sequence so as to eliminate the need to cover reloads. They were slowly advancing. One more Goliath had fallen and the three remaining dinos had danced away from them. The 15 human combatants were now at the corner of the jungle outcropping – only 40 more yards to get to the entrance to Gamma Complex.

Somehow, there was no warning.

Later, they determined that the faceplate HUD had simply overloaded and didn't recognize the new threat. Not until it was too late.

A new Goliath had come screeching out of the thick copse of trees and raked its claws across Nick Jennings's chest, across Anna Tobin's arm and through the back of Wraith soldier Jesse "Alto" Cook. Cadey Park had crash-tackled Anna to the ground as she screamed, looking down at the empty air where her right arm had been.

Anna's environmental suit expanded around the severed limb like a combination of an air-bag and inflatable medical cast. Anna lay on the ground, in shock.

The Wraiths-plus-Damon stopped firing to turn to look at what had happened in their rear ranks. It was then that the three remaining forward Goliaths jumped toward the advancing line. They had been drawing the soldiers closer to the position of their fighter-in-waiting. The Wraiths were sandwiched between two enemies yet again.

Anna and Cadey had rolled out of the way as four of the Wraiths opened fire on the previously hidden Goliath. The other five soldiers turned and began shooting at the onrushing dinos. With the close proximity and the concentrated fire, the ambush Goliath died instantly in a hail of bullets. The four turned immediately and joined in gunning down the three other dinos. The combination of shotguns and assault rifles at close range was devastating. Hux fired his Sledgehammer dry, dropped it and, in one smooth, practiced motion, grabbed his sidearm from a thigh holster. He sighted down the barrel and shot one of the Goliaths directly through the eye.

Ahab was shooting center mass and unloaded his remaining drum into the chest of the center Goliath. Three Wraiths and Damon, with a combination of weaponry, were firing at the last dino who fell, twitching only a yard away from reaching the soldiers.

Beef and Damon rushed to Anna's side. She had passed out from blood loss and shock, but she still had a faint heartbeat.

"We still have her," Cadey said. She was sitting on the ground, cradling Anna's head in her lap. "But not for long."

Not completely trusting the biometric read-out, Ahab was walking to each of the fallen soldiers and scientist and visually inspecting them. He came back to Beef and slowly shook his head. Suddenly, in the distance, they heard a high-pitch roar.

"T-Rex," Anna said.

"Into the trucks," Beef replied.

"They're bad," Damon said. "Broken."

"We ain't got that far to go," Ahab smiled.

CHAPTER 10

THE BIG SWEDE

IT HAD BEEN easier to get inside the two remaining JLTVs and limp them toward the Gamma Complex garage than carry the heavy crates of gear. It was hard to do, but they had ultimately decided to leave their fallen on the battlefield. There had been a significant debate but the impending death of Anna Tobin and the approaching roars of at least two tyrannosaurus rexes – not to mention the other battleground scavengers – sped their decision. Parked in the garage, they were able to unload the gear from the trucks and get everything back to the Objekt 221 facility.

Of course, they had sent Damon, Brighton and Cadey – carrying Anna – back first.

"Remember Christmas," Damon said, standing on the launching pad ready to make the return trip.

"Twelve twenty-five," Alex answered over the faceplate comms from outside the building. "See you on the other side."

* *

There had been a burst of activity as soon as they arrived back at Objekt 221. Anna was rushed off to the facility's medical wing for surgery. Everyone else was taken to the scrub-down and debrief area. Standard operating procedure. SOP. All the storage containers were taken to a clean room for examination and cataloging. It was several hours before the excursion team – what was left of it – was allowed to wander around O221 under their own power.

Ultimately, however, they spent much of the next two days shuttling back and forth from group meetings and individual debriefings that included Angus Pope, AJ Fontana and Joe French from Sergott Solutions – who was mainly interested in Wraith movements and the loss of life that occurred in Ancient Crimea. The sessions broke at regular intervals and the excursion team was allowed to take food breaks or walk around to stretch their legs.

During one such break, Alex and Rick found themselves in a conference room with a catered lunch. In what everyone assumed was a security precaution, the surviving nine Wraith soldiers were largely sequestered to a block of rooms. They were mostly conference rooms – some with kitchenettes and some with cots. The two team leads sat in a corner of one such meeting area. There were two other men in the room – sitting individually.

"That's probably it," Ahab said, wiping his chin with the back of his hand.

Beef Scott nodded, finishing a bite of his sandwich.

"That's the only reason French is here," he said. "We're staying. There must be a secondary mission."

Ahab nodded in return, taking a sip from a can of soda.

"Yep. Did he ask about the aquatic observation deck?" Beef asked.

"Uh huh," Ahab said. "Spent about 20 minutes on it. Spent longer on that than the freakin' shark."

"Yeah."

The two men went silent. Ahab leaned back in his chair; it sagged under his weight.

"You know what I keep thinking about?"

Alex "Beef" Scott shrugged.

"Couldn't even begin to guess," he said.

"There must be a third pad," Ahab paused. "At least."

Scott leaned forward, cocking his head to the side. Ahab remained in his relaxed position. In fact, he let his arms drape over the arms of the chair. So tall was he that his fingertips nearly touched the polished concrete floor.

"Think about it, ace. Those trucks. They came over in one piece. You saw the garage. It was stocked for regular maintenance not the assembly of half a dozen heavy vehicles. There were the two pads in Gamma Complex. How did they get those JLTVs over there?"

"Huh," Alex exclaimed. He rested his elbows on the table surface and rested his chin against his hands. "And the buildings. Even as pre-fab units they would need a huge rift to bring those back. Heck, the glass in those observation rooms looked seamless."

Rick "Ahab" Everson nodded.

"But the rift," Ahab started.

Beef was nodding in return.

"I know," he said. "It's supposed to be like a tunnel. One end here and the other end right in the same spot – just back there. The only thing I can think of …" He paused. "What if what we know of Gamma Complex is just a stair-head? What if there's a huge underground complex with a room-sized pad?"

Ahab made a go-figure motion with his arms. Elbows bent, hands flat, palms up. He shrugged and Beef Scott returned the gesture.

"We might have come here for a simple search and rescue, chum, but this ain't over."

"No," Alex said. "It certainly isn't."

* *

On the same floor but on the opposite end of the wing, Cadey Park and Damon Butcher were also taking a break from a group debriefing – this with Angus Pope. They were sharing a friendly game of foosball. Damon was winning. He had no illusions about the secret "guy code" of always letting the girl win – especially if you were interested in her. He and Cadey had navigated a complex conversation early on in their friendship – a will-they-won't-they discussion.

They weren't ever going to.

Ever.

So, he had decided to kick her butt at foosball yet again. In fact, right now, he was lining up a goal shot from his back two defenders. He fired a shot across the length of the black "grass" of the table and scored.

"You suck," Cadey said, pausing to take a sip of her strawberry lemonade – a specialty of the rec-room bar.

Damon shook his head.

"You only get better by playing a better opponent," he said.

"And stop quoting movies to me," she put the cup down. "Do you think they'll send us back?"

Damon stood up straight, taking his hands off the black rubber handles of the spindles. He put his hands on his lower back and he stretched the muscles there.

"I can't imagine why," he said. "We only had to go back for this fluke event. The rescue mission. It would seem that adventure's over."

Cadey reached down and pulled the hard, white foosball out of the chamber below her goal. She held it in her right hand, paused, thinking.

"Yeah," she said. "I suppose so. But you have to wonder why the team of soldiers are still here. And the lady from corporate. And the new guy from Sergott. Angus and the other department heads were doing fine getting everything up to speed. Why all the extra bodies now?"

"And we did spend a bunch of time at Hell Island clearing out digital storage." Damon cracked his neck from side to side. "Wonder what was in those files."

Cadey shrugged.

"The idea that Facility Four was performing genetic modifications on dinosaurs is a little creepy. I'm fairly certain that

Goliath wasn't the only experiment." She paused for a moment, looking at the ball. "Didn't they call the Goliath *Experiment 47?*"

Damon leaned forward and put his palms flat on the top edge of the table. He leaned toward Cadey and adopted a conspiratorial tone.

"And what's with that underwater observation lab?" he asked. "What were they looking at?"

Cadey shrugged again. She reached forward to drop the foosball into the slot to start the next point.

"I get the sense that we're going to find out shortly," she said and dropped the ball into the field of play. "Like it or not."

* *

The surgical staff was basically made up of Allied Genetics medical personnel. Many of the workers at Objekt 221 were vetted AG employees. The security and HR staff were keeping tabs on them, but nearly 40 percent of the workers who were at O221 when the hostile takeover took place still worked at the facility – under the control of Precision Robotics.

Anna Tobin was going to be just fine.

She was beginning the long path toward recovery. They hadn't been able to save her arm, but she was being fitted for prosthetics right now. Davis Brighton hadn't left her side since they came back from Ancient Crimea. He had a shouting match in the hallway with Angus Pope when Davis missed a debriefing session.

Anna was still weak from the initial blood loss, but she was awake and she was out of danger. The consultant had left after taking various measurements of Anna's left arm. He was the senior tech in the synth lab of Precision Robotics's Sunnyvale, California, facility. James Caufield. With a nod to Davis, James left the room.

Davis slid a chair over next to Anna's bed.

"Twelve down," he said and smiled. Anna returned the smile and leaned her head back against the stack of pillows.

"Yeah," she said. "So, about half. Potentially."

Davis nodded.

"Assuming there was no reproduction," he said. "Or, natural attrition. God forbid. I suppose it's possible that some other predator got lucky and beat one."

"Possible but not likely," Anna said, closing her eyes. "Do they know about the other facilities?"

"I'm not sure," Davis said. "I handed over what data I could, but I kept back some files. I'm not sure what they might have uncovered here at 221. I guess we'll have to play it by ear."

"Well, they know that Hell Island was technically Facility Four … but they won't know where to start counting. Maybe 221 is Facility One, you know?"

"Right. Can we trust them?"

"No," Anna said, her eyes snapping open. "They attacked this facility and trapped us back there for over four months. We lost Nick, Art and Cove. Plus security."

"Okay, okay." Davis patted her knee. "We can assume they'll uncover the facilities. I'm sure there's a map here somewhere. This Pope fella seems smart – if a bit too trusting. We should also assume they'll start uncovering the other experimental hybrids."

Anna leaned her head back and again closed her eyes. Davis could almost see the energy draining from her.

"Yeah," she said, a throaty whisper. "You're probably right. Maybe we'll get lucky and the O47s and O48s will just kill each other. Then we just get to deal with the . . ."

And, just like that, she was snoring.

Davis sat for a minute and watched her sleep. He stood up and gave her a sad, crooked smile.

"Yeah," he said, turning to leave the room. "Maybe we'll get lucky."

* *

Angus Pope had started referring to AJ as "The Big Swede." There was nothing about her that suggested that particular heritage and it wasn't a negative or derogative phrase in Pope's mind. It was just a descriptor. In fact, he got a kick out of AJ Fontana. He might ask her out when everything had calmed down.

She had jetted out of their final meeting of the day after a quick goodbye. Maybe she was already sweet on someone else. Angus shrugged to himself and made a soft sound in the back of his throat that was something close to "mlem," but nobody had heard him. He was walking over to his office – the former office of the operational director of Objekt 221. Britta something. Vragi. Britta Vragi.

He had heard that a grenade had gone off in the room, but they had done a nice job putting everything back together. Except the desk. There was no desk. Just a table.

Angus pushed open the heavy mahogany door and walked into the office. He had a stack of paperwork under his right arm and he shoved the door closed with his left. The plan was to put the paperwork away and then go grab dinner. They had a big group meeting tomorrow morning to lay out their plans for the facility, the rift and Ancient Crimea. Not everyone was going to be happy about it. He wanted a quiet evening to gather his thoughts.

He put the paperwork down on the desk – what was essentially a dining room table – and sat down in the oversized red tufted-leather chair in the far corner of the room. Angus pushed his glasses up past his forehead to rest them across the top of his head. He rubbed the corners of his eyes with the fingertips from both hands.

When he opened his eyes, he was greeted with the customary blurred vision. He was looking around and something caught his eye. Something he had never seen before. He pulled his glasses back down and looked at the wood molding around the built-in bookcase just past his right shoulder. There was a black button the size of a dime pressed up against the bottom shelf of the bookcase. You could only see the button while sitting in this chair in this position with the lights just so. Otherwise, it would be in shadow.

"Hello there," Angus said.

He reached forward with his left index finger and pressed the button.

Like something out of a James Bond movie, the entire bookcase slid to the right, exposing 20 small LCD screens mounted on the wall. As the bookcase finished its movement, a keyboard dropped into position right in front of him, attached to a swivel-arm at the bottom-left-most screen. The screen closest to the keyboard had a tiny text cursor in the upper left of the monitor. It was blinking as if waiting for some sort of input. Angus pressed the ENTER key on the keyboard. The cursor changed to:

ACTIVE? Y/N

"Okay," Angus said and shrugged.

He pressed the Y key. Nineteen of the monitors reacted with the word NULL in the cursor position. The topmost monitor on the left, however, began a read-out of complex graphs, lines and numbers. Angus stood to read it.

"Vital signs," he said.

Across the top of the screen was the name:

GRIFF ADAMS

And then the line below that:

SARGE

"No way," Angus said.

There was still a survivor in Ancient Crimea.

Angus reached into his pocket and grabbed his cell phone. He pressed the speed-dial contact for his counterpart at the Sunnyvale office. He was the next in line to come and supervise the operation at Objekt 221.

"You're not going to believe this, Jerry," he said, smiling.

It only took seconds for the smile to fade completely.

"Okay," Angus said, adopting a more serious tone. "Send me what you decrypted of the conversations. I'll go talk to French right now and see about getting it all sorted out."

* *

AJ Fontana had hurried away from the meeting room. Her quarters were at the end of the wing and down one floor. It struck her again how huge this facility was – especially when you were in a hurry. The poor-man's definition of relativity.

She was polite to the people she passed – a nod here, a smile there. Two people had tried to stop her for a conversation. She grinned apologetically and tapped her wristwatch.

"Later," she said both times. Verbatim. "I promise."

She entered her room and put down her purse and folio on the coffee table. She had been given a suite – similar to an American hotel suite. There was a bed and a small wall dividing off the sitting area with a television and couch. She walked through this half of the room, through the section that represented the bedroom and walked into the bathroom. She sat on the edge of the tub – it was an oddly luxurious tub – and took off her shoes. She was wearing black flats with a thicker-than-average sole. On the bottom of the right shoe was an intricate design indicating the European manufacturer. She leaned back and pulled a handful of change out of her left hip pocket. Even though she never bought anything with cash, she always seemed to have 47 cents in her pocket. A quarter. Two dimes. Two pennies. She took one of the dimes and slid it into the manufacturer's imprint on the sole.

It locked into place with a magnetic snap. The elevated heel slid over to reveal a small piece of electronics. Essentially, it was a texting machine. The face had a small green screen with 10 buttons – one for each digit. She smiled, pretending she was sending a text message in 1998. Press the number 2 three times to finally reach the letter C, and so on. At least it was set up with predictive text – T9.

EXCURSION BACK. NO DATA ON ENERGY SOURCE.

She pressed SEND and sat back a bit waiting for a reply. There were four security cameras in her O221 suite, but none in the bathroom. At least none she could find. She still worried that there was one in here somewhere, but she couldn't find it. And no one had come to snatch her up after what she'd been doing in here for four days.

A reply flashed on the screen.

NOT AT RUINS?

She immediately tapped out NEGATIVE and sent the message.

MUST BE CLOSE.

She thought for a moment, running through the map of all the facilities and the various vestiges of the ancient civilization they had uncovered.

POSSIBLY BUILDING 5.

It was a short wait for the next message.

SARGE FAILED.

YES, she replied.

DID HE ELIMINATE WITNESSES?

NEGATIVE, she replied.

It was tedious to talk this way, but they couldn't risk the data stream for an actual conversation. This was the best way to stay under the radar.

THEY FOUND FACILITY 4?

AFFIRMATIVE.

AQUATIC LAB?

NO DATA, she typed.

FIND ENERGY SOURCE.

It felt like a final message. She waited and then typed out PROJECT JENI CONFIRMED.

GOOD. WE WILL LOCATE.

And then the little machine was silent.

She put the texting machine back in her heel, reattached the heel to her shoe and put her shoes back on. AJ stood up and exited the room with a wry smile on her face.

"If you want something done right," she said to the room in general, "you gotta do it yourself."

THE END

AFTERWORD

THE MYSTERIOUS ENERGY SOURCE

A RESCUE MISSION. The idea was intriguing. I had wanted to write a follow-up to **Objekt 221**, but wasn't sure which direction to go. I could focus on Allied Genetics. I could focus on Precision Robotics. I could focus on the Wraiths. I could focus on Damon or Cadey. I could focus on the dinos. I could focus on Humanity 1.0. There was enough raw material in that story to drive many others.

But, a rescue mission. That might be cool. It would give me a way to bring all of those elements back together for another short adventure. Explore Ancient Crimea just a little more. The problem was, well, the simple rescue mission story sort of … well it just sort of spiraled out of control. AJ Fontana. Sarge. The aquatic observation chamber hidden beneath Facility Four. 047 AND 048. Joe French. The rescue mission became a sort of launching pad all on its own. There's a LOT more about Allied Genetics that we didn't know about. How many facilities ARE there? Where is the mysterious energy source? Are there more ruins?

Might be fun to dig a little deeper.

In fact, the third story is already in the early planning stages. It's tentatively titled "The Dinosaur Ruins," but we'll see. Working titles have a way of morphing as a story takes shape. This one might be a bit longer, though. I feel that there has been quite a bit of set-up to this point and I'm going to need to pay off a bunch of those teases. The entire final chapter of this story, for example, serves as a summary to all the unanswered questions that have been brought up.

* *

Thank you all, kind readers, for getting through this story. I'm sure many – if not all of you – have also read **Objekt 221**. I hope you've enjoyed both. They were both great fun to write. And if you've spent any time exploring "creative writing land," you know that's not always the case. Some stories are a joy to write and some are pure anguish. Both this story and O221, though, were a pleasure to go back and read through. I hope you've had as much fun as I did.

I've always joked that my stories all take place in the same universe. In truth, most stories contain some sort of sly nod or crossover to another work. Angus Pope actually first appeared in the short story "Machine Reality" in the collection **The Event: Precision Robotics**. I mention that Arlington Beech was hired away from Tate McKenna – a main character in the novel-in-progress **Phoenix Hill**. Let me know if you saw others. There might be a couple more …

* *

Feel free to reach out to me with any questions or comments … or if you just want to see what I'm working on. I'm on most social media outlets as well as the inconsistently-updated www.steve-metcalf.com

Keep reading. Keep writing.

Steve Metcalf

June 27th, 2020

Leander, Texas

Also By Steve Metcalf
RESET: A Videogame Anecdote
Sketch
The Beast of Trash Island
Objekt 221

King Paranormal Investigations Series
Coldwater
The Hidden Riches of Lord Granite
Paradox Iron

Collections
The Event: The Chicago Rust Yards
The Event: Iron Bay
The Event: Precision Robotics
The Event: Gold Rush

CHECK OUT OTHER GREAT
DINOSAUR THRILLERS

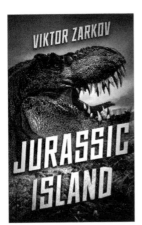

JURASSIC ISLAND
by Viktor Zarkov

Guided by satellite photos and modern technology a ragtag group of survivalists and scientists travel to an uncharted island in the remote South Indian Ocean. Things go to hell in a hurry once the team reaches the island and the massive megalodon that attacked their boats is only the beginning of their desperate fight for survival.

Nothing could have prepared billionaire explorer Joseph Thornton and washed up archaeologist Christopher "Colt" McKinnon for the terrifying prehistoric creatures that wait for them on JURASSIC ISLAND!

K-REX
by L.Z. Hunter

Deep within the Congo jungle, Circuitz Mining employs mercenaries as security for its Coltan mining site. Armed with assault rifles and decades of experience, nothing should go wrong. However, the dangers within the jungle stretch beyond venomous snakes and poisonous spiders. There is more to fear than guerrillas and vicious animals. Undetected, something lurks under the expansive treetop canopy . . .

Something ancient.

Something dangerous.

Kasai Rex!

CHECK OUT OTHER GREAT DINOSAUR THRILLERS

WRITTEN IN STONE
by David Rhodes

Charles Dawson is trapped 100 million years in the past. Trying to survive from day to day in a world of dinosaurs he devises a plan to change his fate. As he begins to write messages in the soft mud of a nearby stream, he can only hope they will be found by someone who can stop his time travel. Professor Ron Fontana and Professor Ray Taggit, scientists with opposing views, each discover the fossilized messages. While attempting to save Charles, Professor Fontana, his daughter Lauren and their friend Danny are forced to join Taggit and his group of mercenaries. Taggit does not intend to rescue Charles Dawson, but to force Dawson to travel back in time to gather samples for Taggit's fame and fortune. As the two groups jump through time they find they must work together to make it back alive as this fast-paced thriller climaxes at the very moment the age of dinosaurs is ending.

HARD TIME
by Alex Laybourne

Rookie officer Peter Malone and his heavily armed team are sent on a deadly mission to extract a dangerous criminal from a classified prison world. A Kruger Correctional facility where only the hardest, most vicious criminals are sent to fend for themselves, never to return.

But when the team come face to face with ancient beasts from a lost world, their mission is changed. The new objective: Survive.

CHECK OUT OTHER GREAT DINOSAUR THRILLERS

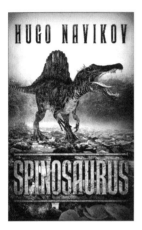

SPINOSAURUS
by Hugo Navikov

Brett Russell is a hunter of the rarest game. His targets are cryptids, animals denied by science. But they are well known by those living on the edges of civilization, where monsters attack and devour their animals and children and lay ruin to their shantytowns.

When a shadowy organization sends Brett to the Congo in search of the legendary dinosaur cryptid Kasai Rex, he will face much more than a terrifying monster from the past. Spinosaurus is a dinosaur thriller packed with intrigue, action and giant prehistoric predators.

LAND OF DEATH
by Eric S Brown & Alex Laybourne

A group of American soldiers, fleeing an organized attack on their base camp in the Middle East, encounter a storm unlike anything they've seen before. When the storm subsides, they wake up to find themselves no longer in the desert and perhaps not even on Earth. The jungle they've been deposited in is a place ruled by prehistoric creatures long extinct. Each day is a struggle to survive as their ammo begins to run low and virtually everything they encounter, in this land they've been hurled into, is a deadly threat.

Printed in Great Britain
by Amazon